*In Memory of*

JAMES GURNEY

by

his wife

1994

# AN INCH OF FORTUNE

## Simon Raven

Blond & Briggs

First published in Great Britain 1980
by Blond & Briggs Ltd, London NW2 6LE

British Library Cataloguing in Publication Data

Raven, Simon
    An inch of fortune.
    I. Title
    823'.9'1F      PR6068.A91/

ISBN 0–85634–108–8

Printed in Great Britain by The Anchor Press Ltd
and bound by Wm Brendon & Son Ltd
both of Tiptree, Essex

# Preface

In the summer of 1950 I was employed, during much of the Long Vacation, as bear-leader to the erratic and erotic son of an hysterical millionairess. The more satyr-like wagged the son, the more volatile waxed the mother, and vice versa : and so the thing went on, in a quite unstoppable spiral, gyrating ever faster and fiercer, until the day I got the sack for failing to give proper account of my expenditure on Master Cherubino's laundry at the Grand Hotel du Palais in Biarritz, whither my employer had propelled us because the Windsors and Elsa Maxwell were to be there for the season.

Back home and in deep disgrace with the tutor of my college (who had procured the job for me through the college solicitors in the hope, now absolutely undone, that I might pay my Buttery bill), I settled down to spend the rest of the Long Vacation, which should have been dedicated to Plato, in turning my cockayne summer into a novel. By November the tale was finished, professionally typed (on credit) and titled : *A Passage to Biarritz* I called it, in the hope of annoying an Honorary Fellow of my college called E. M. (Morgan) Forster, whom I toadied with the rest but secretly considered to be an idle, pampered, sanctimonious and spiteful old man, pathologically mean with money and for ever sucking up to the working class.

I submitted my novel to my friend Roger Lubbock of Putnam (London), who very properly refused to publish it on the ground that it was libellous. I had barely troubled, as he pointed out, even to change people's names. Well, I said, would Putnam, as a handsome gesture to an aspirant author, at least foot the typist's bill? No, Putnam wouldn't (and serve me right for my nasty thoughts about Morgan Forster). But what Putnam *might* do would be to reconsider the book, if I would take it away and rewrite it, altering place, time, incident and nomenclature to a point where the thing could begin to be called fiction.

To complete the first version I had scanted my studies of Plato : to complete the second I now totally neglected my Fellowship Dissertation. I was not born to be a Scholar, I told myself, but a Man of Letters – which would pay a great deal better. In the intervals of writing novel reviews for *The Listener* (a job I had obtained as a reward for amusing Morgan's friend J. R. Ackerley, the Literary Editor, with scabrous stories about Morgan) I laboured to bring *A Passage to Biarritz* within the bounds of publishable propriety. And by the Christmas of 1951 there it was, my *lepidum novom libellum, modo expolitum*, newly re-pumiced in text and texture, re-titled *An Inch of Fortune*, and all ready for re-inspection by Roger Lubbock of Putnam.

Roger liked it; a contract was about to issue; a cheque for £50 (enormous wealth in those days) was as good as in the post – when Roger's superior, a long, costive, creaking number called Huntington, a kind of thin-skinned crocodile, developed cold feet. The book was still, he said, libellous, although the lady (to my mind) had been clothed in seven veils, and Venice (which I had visited for the first time the previous April) substituted for Biarritz. None of this sufficed for Huntington. Defamatory, he said; and in any case far too brash and very, very lewd. But of course, if Raven would care to take it away and rewrite it . . . Raven would not. He had had enough, if only for the time, of being a Man of Letters, and had decided on a preliminary career of action instead : after all, it would pay a great deal better. As indeed, though indirectly, it did. Five years with the Regular Army in Africa and Europe were a far better introduction to both life and letters than hanging round Grub Street, which is what I should have done had my novel been accepted; and the bustle of camp and tavern was in every way more invigorating and educative than fugging in King's College, Cambridge, while it rotted to pieces of tertiary socialism, which would have been my lot had I been invited to continue my academic career. As things were, when the time came for me to leave the Army (slow horses), I had a world I could write about and a style I could write in, this being rooted in the Army's common sense and unrivalled rule of composition – 'Be Brief, Neat and Plain.' And so I conclude that it was a good thing that I

6

abandoned my Dissertation for my novel and an even better thing that I abandoned my novel to go for a soldier. But what of the book itself, *An Inch of Fortune*? What happened to that?

It vanished altogether. What remained and still remains is the original book, *A Passage to Biarritz,* which had been renamed *An Inch of Fortune* for working purposes even before I began to revise it and should, I think, retain that title now.

Rejected by Putnam, by Roger Lubbock and the scaly Huntington, rejected even by traitorous me, it yet survived at the bottom of tin trunks and cricket bags, in cellars and in baggage holds and under the stairs of distressful lodgings, until one day it surfaced from beneath a pile of Racing Calendars and Loeb editions of Plato's Dialogues. A clear sign from the gods that it was time to attend to it again; so I gave it to Anthony Blond of Anthony Blond Ltd. (as it then was), who forgot to read it. Again the poor battered manuscript descended into the underworld, but somehow travelled as the firm travelled, from Chester Row to Doughty Street to Caroline Place to Museum Street . . . where, at long last, as Blond & Briggs Ltd was preparing to remove for the final time, it came to light once more and was for the first occasion in twenty-eight years, positively and sympathetically read.

Libellous it is no longer (if ever it was), for one cannot libel the dead. Brash it still is, I admit; lewd it still is, I fancy; but in any case at all, or so at least I have been sincerely assured, it is vigorous and it is funny. I very much hope some few, or even some many, may find it so. For it takes me back to my spunky youth, when I first went to Biarritz thirty years ago, saw Elsa Maxwell plain and even bowed to Wallis Windsor.

S.R.

Venice 1980

*Iras*        Am I not of fortune better
than she?
*Charmian*   Well, if you were but an
inch of fortune better than I,
where would you choose it?
*Iras*        Not in my husband's nose.

*Antony and Cleopatra*, William Shakespeare

# I

So here one was, thought Esme, excitement over, tears shed, excuses and promises judiciously inserted, sitting in a train on the dirtiest line in England at four o'clock on the hottest afternoon of the summer. This was what came of extravagance. All his friends seemed to receive last-minute cheques on these occasions, with implied permission to repeat the whole performance. All he had received was a card, which said Mr E. S. Sa Foy was requested to call on the Bursar at seven o'clock on Wednesday. When he had done so, there had been five minutes of otiose discussion (why did he spend money he hadn't got?) followed up by what was on first appearances an even more otiose discussion on the subject of ways and means. His means, it had soon been discovered, were palpably inadequate to the occasion; but it was only when the conversation had been brought round to ways that the full horror of the situation had become evident.

'So what it amounts to,' said the Bursar with intensity, 'is this. The full amount of your debt to this college is something over two hundred pounds. You are due to take your degree in a year, by which time this bill – as well as next year's – must be paid. You receive your usual allowance in July, and apart from this you have nothing at all.'

'That's right,' said Esme.

'I therefore propose – and not merely for the sake of argument – the following arrangement. By July 15 you will give me a cheque for three-quarters of the sum you are due to receive – which will work out at sixty pounds. By September 15 you will produce a further sixty pounds, and as you will not be in residence during the Long Vacation, the quarterly allowance on your scholarship will realize yet another twenty-five. All this will account for nearly a hundred and fifty, which is a good start at any rate.'

'But where,' said Esme, 'am I to get sixty pounds to give you on September 15?'

'I was coming to that,' said the Bursar. 'Presuming even your capacity for borrowing money without qualm or security has by now lost much of its edge, it only remains that you should make some. In order to save sixty pounds you will have to make a good deal. I therefore propose blindfolding my conscience and recommending you for a job – this job,' he said, passing a disagreeable-looking letter, 'so please read that.'

Esme read it.

Dear Sir, (it said)

I am writing on behalf of my client, who prefers, for the time being, to remain anonymous.

She is looking for a young man, of good intelligence and a responsible attitude, to act as tutor to her eldest adopted son. This boy is at present at school in Switzerland, having been involved in an unfortunate set of circumstances which made it necessary for him to leave Eton at the age of fourteen and a half.

He returns for his summer holiday on July 5, and will be in this country until the beginning of September. The tutor would be engaged for the whole of this period, his salary would be high, and all his expenses, including laundry, paid.

His duties would not involve teaching anything to the boy, but he would be required to accompany him constantly, to check any attempts at action of an anti-social nature, and above all to watch for any tendencies towards psychopathic behaviour.

If you have in mind a young man of suitable disposition who is prepared to undertake such employment, I should be much obliged if you would communicate with me. All information given in this letter is kindly to be regarded as strictly confidential.

I am, sir,
Yours truly,
Frederick Gower,
of Gower, Constantine and Gower Ltd,
Solicitors.

'Well?' said the Bursar.

'I imagine my intelligence is good enough.'

'And your attitude, your disposition?'

'At least I wasn't sacked at fourteen and a half.'

'But you were at seventeen and a half, and in circumstances so discreditable and disgusting that even you have not boasted of the fact to more than about half your friends.'

'That was a long time ago,' said Esme without conviction.

'And the little incident that nearly led to your being deprived of your commission?'

'That was only slackness – an oversight, nothing fundamentally disgraceful.'

'But most certainly unsatisfactory. Now let's get this straight, Esme. I happen to like you, and there's no doubt that every now and again you do us all credit – more by accident than design of course, but you still do us credit. There was that prize, and your First, and the favourable impression you made on the Warden of Wadham. Against these, there is the incident at Bolsover's twenty-first birthday party, the limerick about the President, the time you borrowed the Treasurer's Bentley, and, above all, this persistent and enormous debt – which in any case is probably a mere thimbleful of weak tea when compared with others you owe in the town and to friends. So what happens? We like you, we mean to keep you, but if only you'd just pretend to make the tiniest effort to pay the merest fraction of your bill, it would be so encouraging. But you haven't, you won't, and you say you can't.

'So I'm finding you a job. But this letter is from the firm that also handle the college affairs, their client is certain to be well known, and if there's even so much as the merest sniff of an incident, I'll have you transferred to Liverpool for ever. So there,' said the Bursar.

'But I haven't got the job yet.'

'All I can say is you'd better get it. I've written to the head of the firm with a personal recommendation of you – your abilities, your understanding, your tact and your social address. If they don't examine your past record you'll hear from them soon enough. So that, for the time being, is that. Now if you'll please go away, taking your bill with you as a little reminder of the trouble you've caused, I'd be much obliged. And, Esme,' said the Bursar, 'please, please, please, NO INCIDENTS.'

That had been a week ago. Five days later Esme had had a

telegram, which said, 'Telephone WEL 4464 re tutoring Terence Fox. McTavish.' So he had borrowed half-a-crown in sixpences from the Bursar, and had been curtly told that Dr McTavish was out on a case but had left word for Mr Sa Foy to ring Badlock 412 (wherever Badlock might be, thought Esme, as he hurried off to touch the Bursar for another half-crown) where he could speak in person, to the Honourable Mrs Sandra Fairweather, his prospective employer it appeared.

The 'phone was answered by a throaty, empire-building sort of voice, presumably but not incontestably feminine.

'I want to speak to the Honourable Mrs Sandra Fairweather,' said Esme.

'Mrs Fairweather speaking,' said the voice, as though the sun never set on it.

'Oh. Yes. This is Mr Sa Foy here. I think – '

'Who?' said the voice.

'Mr Sa Foy. I – '

'Hurry up,' said the voice, 'my dog's just gone on the carpet and if I don't hit it now, it'll forget why.'

'Mr McTavish, that is Dr McTavish, said I was to r—'

'Oh, it's Mr Sa Foy, you might have said so. When can you come and be interviewed? Badlock's no way at all from Cambridge, and the car can meet you at the station. Whatever I think of you it'll be worth the journey, because I can show you my borders – they're magnificent just now, a great stinking mess, by Heaven, it might have been a horse. Will tomorrow do? McTavish will be here – and a sick friend of mine from London who may die – you won't mind that? – he's done it all over the place.'

'It sounds very pleasant. What time?'

'Five-thirty at the station. As I say, McTavish will be here. He's made a stench like a sewer. I'll teach you to shit. Good-bye, Mr Sa Foy.'

'Good-bye,' said Esme.

Esme Sangrail Sa Foy was twenty-two years old and came of a totally obscure family. (Heaven alone knew where his name had come from.) But his paternal grandfather had been very rich and his father, though the youngest son, had not been poor. The pity of course was that Esme's mother, who adored him, had never possessed a penny. Indeed that was thoroughly typical of his

14

fortune all round. His godfathers were perpetually dying intestate, while his maternal grandmother, who worshipped him, had become a very rich woman due to the death of a cousin – but only a week before she herself gave up the ghost, in consequence of which she had not had time to alter her will. But as Esme, who was then nineteen, had remarked, one was beginning to expect this kind of thing; and indeed it was just as well he received an early inoculation.

His father was a futile and embittered man who had spent all his life pretending to look for a suitable occupation. Since he had £2,000 a year of his own it had to be exactly suitable – which, after the first month, no occupation ever was. So he developed a grudge about the difficulty of life on £2,000 a year and the general lack of suitability, for a man of his type, of every known occupation, and settled down to play round after round of golf in order to preserve his appetite – which was quite unnecessary, as he was in any case an inordinately greedy man. After he was forty-five he could neither play so well nor so often (age and the war having taken their toll of himself and his companions), with the result that, while his appetite was unimpaired, he became more embittered than ever. In after years Esme would measure his own transition from childhood through adolescence and to man's estate not so much by time or by incident as by the increasing disagreeableness of his father ('that was the year when he thought he had an ulcer').

But for all this, Esme's education had been a good one. He started it at a smart, finicky and expensive Surrey prep school. After he had been there four years the war and a major scandal (which included Esme) brought this to an end, and he was hurried off to safety (both physical and moral) in Somerset. There he was taught Greek, a subject for which the first school had been too modern, and found himself, in the summer of 1941, elected to the top entrance scholarship of a large and important public school known as Mandata Domus.

On arrival there the following September he learnt three things which had so far been carefully concealed from him. The first was that he must be extremely clever, as scholars in general and top scholars in particular were not elected for looks; and the second was that, if they had been elected for looks, he would still have won a good place. He found these two items very encouraging : and when he considered them in conjunction with the third thing he now learnt, which was an unedited version of the facts of life, he felt that there was a vista before him of almost infinite variety and diversion.

He was right. There was. But there was also, he discovered, a class of men whose life's work it was to prevent people enjoying that vista. Every year more people discovered, like himself, that it was there, and every year the self-appointed vigilants gathered themselves together with more determination than ever to fulfil their proper function as pedagogues, which was, first and so far as in them lay, to obscure the attractions of the prospect, and secondly, where this was impossible, to denounce it as a sinful vision. (It was their way of getting their own back for the inadequacy of their salaries.) Now as the country was involved, when Esme first arrived, in a large and destructive war, and as the men who proffered their services as schoolmasters were in consequence more decrepit than usual, one would have thought they would have had their hands fully occupied with the more profitable business of educating the young rather than with that of afflicting them with their own inhibitions. But not a bit of it. If their hands were more palsied, their denunciations, at the same time, were more impassioned, their watch was more vigilant, and their interference with everybody's amusements was more indefatigable than at any previous time. They even had a new weapon. For in peace-time interference had been conducted in the name of class, morals and, of course, the founder (who was supposed to represent both, but was in fact a revolting Elizabethan profiteer who had sought to cleanse his soul by dispensing a fraction of his ill-gotten fortune in the cause of education): but it was now discovered that the sanction of war could be used for an appeal to 'the old boys in the trenches', whose deaths were accordingly recited at evensong every Sunday. To this appeal, as was rightly thought, only the most corrupt souls could remain deaf; so that Sunday evening was a time of guilt, unhappiness and trembling, for one had just heard solemnly recited the names of twenty men, now dead, whose sacrifice, it appeared, one had profaned and sullied by all the short comings, irreverance and ingratitude one's own recent conduct had displayed. It was an unpleasant charge, and few boys had either the intelligence or the courage to withstand it. Life at school during the war was therefore dull, hag-ridden, uncomfortable, and, above all, deadened by that deplorable opiate, a sense of guilt.

Esme's reaction to all this was immediate and, for his years, commendable. He decided first that it would stand him in good stead to work hard and learn as much as possible; and secondly, that on every other score he would do his best to cheat the grudging crowd who wished to curtail his enjoyments. To this end he reckoned his strongest weapon was deceit, for it would have the incomparable advantage of bringing him positions of credit and responsibility, the abuse of which would be a final and unequalled pleasure.

For a time all went well, and his excellent work received all the commendation it deserved. The trouble came over what people called his character; for while his deceits were woven into a tissue of ingenious device, his natural vanity, combined with a keen sense of humour, prevented him from keeping the necessary silence when a master-stroke had been achieved. What made it worse was that he included among his butts things held practically sacred in time of war, things like the School O.T.C., National Service, God, and the House Spirit – all of which seemed to him merely rather crude excuses for curtailing his (already quite cultured) leisure and interfering with his physical comfort. The usual jingle (able but unstable) began to go the rounds.

Oddly enough, however, his acknowledged irresponsibility, far from keeping him in mean positions, seemed actually to contribute to the swiftness of his promotion. The explanation was twofold and very simple. In the first place, he had the great gift of confessing his sins, with the utmost ingenuousness and with apparent shame, just when (as he very well knew) he was about to be summoned and called to account. (His technique in promising new starts was unrivalled.) And secondly, his house-master had a firm nineteenth-century belief in the essential goodness of all intelligent people – provided, of course, their intelligence was not allowed to become atrophied. It followed therefore that if an intelligent person like Esme was misbehaving, it was due to his having inadequate opportunity for the exercise of his gifts. This delusion he himself was not slow to encourage. Among Oxford men, it seems, the belief about man loving the highest dies hard : for even three and a half years of Esme were not taken as confutation.

The upshot of it all was that in September of 1945, Esme found himself a foundation scholar of a well-known Cambridge college, assistant head-monitor of his house, and with a year to kill before leaving school. For it had been decided that to send him straight to Cambridge at seventeen and a half would not give the opportunity for the final development that was required of his moral backbone. A further year at school, it was hopefully assumed, with even greater responsibilities, would at last take care of that. Nobody had yet realized that in Esme's case the moral backbone, like the appendix, had been in a condition of desuetude from birth.

As for Esme himself, he had decided that after four years' genuine hard work this last should be spent in cultured relaxation. As the war was now over no one could really object to culture (though even over this there was a good deal of muttering); it was Esme's ideas of relaxation (opportunities for which in his present position of trust were almost unlimited) that really did him in. One day the monitor next beneath him, who stood to inherit his position, after overhearing a particularly scabrous series of uproarious confessions, persuaded himself that the path of duty was plain and led to the house-master's study.

Esme was summoned without delay. He employed his confessional charm as never before, he promised new starts of Arctic severity and Utopian cleanliness, he even said he would get confirmed. But for once he had gone too far. His parents appeared on the following day: and Esme was taken away, tearful but unregenerate, to the accompaniment of a chorus he was often to hear again – 'I always said that boy was heading for a bad end.'

Somehow or other he came through the Army with his reputation slightly mended. A War Office Selection Board was deceived by his good manners, and he had been despatched to an Officers' Training School in India. Here it was reckoned impossible to fail one's commission, as too much public money had been spent on getting one there for the most incompetent cadet to be allowed to return ungazetted. Esme, furthermore, made up to his platoon officer by pretending to be ill but refusing to go sick, in consequence of which he was excused unpleasant tasks and received an excellent report.

True, there had been a little incident on his return. For while he had been lucky enough to be commissioned into an extremely smart regiment, his first colonel had been shrewd enough to classify him as he deserved, and had had him attached to a regiment of Artillery – and an inferior one at that. One day an inspecting brigadier found rust on one of his guns. The Commanding Officer sent for him, and remarked rather tartly that he had promised the regiment a half-holiday if the inspection went off well : due to Esme it hadn't, and the half-holiday was therefore cancelled. What, enquired Esme, had been wrong? There had been rust, that was what had been wrong, on Mr Sa Foy's second gun. 'But, sir,' entreated Esme, 'I'm sure it was only a very little rust' – a reply considered insolent in the extreme. Esme was allowed to retain his commission, but thereafter to do very little more than carry unimportant despatches from Larkhill to Salisbury. This suited him very well, as it was both unexacting and provided variety; but his final report was equivocal, and after all that occurred it was only by a hair's breadth that his college allowed him to come up.

But come up he did (after all, they said, he had been commissioned), explaining to all his friends that he was now receiving another chance, approximately his hundredth, and they must really not encourage him to misbehave. Now as luck would have it, he had spotted his father in the act of falsifying his income-tax return and had thereupon blackmailed him into providing a very adequate allowance. Against this, he had developed a new tendency (precluded, of course, at school but encouraged by the Army) towards extremely lavish expenditure in the matter of food and drink. To do him justice he had a gift and a passion for entertaining that afforded as much pleasure to others as expense to himself. And indeed for a year all went well, for he had returned to his old habit of hard work, and a twenty-first birthday so far increased his annual income that the adverse balance for the twelve-month was no more than a mere two or three hundred pounds. On this occasion he received a cheque and a final warning.

It was his second year that provided at once his justification and his indictment. For in the course of it he won a university prize, took a very passable First, spent more money than ever, and didn't have a twenty-first birthday. Throughout the year his overall debt had been mounting steadily : his father, who had now decided that honesty was the best policy where income-tax was concerned, remained severely indifferent : and the Bursar of his college, a kindly man, accepted with increasing reluctance, throughout the autumn, the winter and the spring, a series of plausible explanations of delay and apologetic promises of not too distant payment. But by the middle of the summer he felt he had borne enough. Meanwhile the unrepentant Esme gave a large and satisfactory party to celebrate his First, and was on the verge of disappearing, without leaving an address, to spend a tasteful vacation with (and off) a woman of his acquaintance, when he was summoned by the Bursar and treated as we have seen. It was too bad. Had the note come twelve hours later it would have come too late. Esme had stamped and raved but there was no help for it. The Cambridge–Badlock train contrasted unfavourably with the Golden Arrow.

# II

So here he was at Badlock station and with half-an-hour to kill before Mrs Fairweather's car could be expected. 'Tea,' he thought, left the station, and turned into the main street at the traffic lights. Here he was encouraged to find that alternate signs said alcohol and tea, while an unpretentious church tower at the end of the street looked as though it had been a silent witness of long standing to the excellence and indispensability of both. What a nice place, said Esme to himself, a nice, dreamy, Trollopy – that is, Trollopean – sort of place, where I'm sure it is always tea-time.

The first café he came to was unambiguously shut and in a state of decay as well. He passed the Red Lion, the Green Dragon and the Duke of Panton (coach-house) and was told in the second café that teas had ceased to pay off in Badlock, as all the natives had it at home to save money and no outsider ever stopped. In a minute or two he began to understand why. Could he get cigarettes? he asked. They supposed so, they said, as if everyone in Badlock had given up smoking. Well where? They didn't seem rightly to know the answer, but perhaps – no, not there – perhaps somewhere else: he'd see the sign. Fenland mentality, thought Esme, inbreeding, very John Caldigate, not a bit Barchester. The sun went in as though in agreement with him, and the place began to look more like the ghost-town it rightfully was, the unattractive graveyard of the prosperity it had known in the days when the Cam was a wealthy trade-river and the wares of all Europe were sold on its banks.

Ungay, thought Esme, and found he could only buy the worst possible cigarettes – a transaction which took all of ten minutes, since any native who entered the shop was accorded instant priority, even though he himself was in the middle of his purchase.

And unfriendly, he added to himself, without bothering to count the change and thereby being defrauded of one and sixpence.

But things looked brighter again when he returned to the station (still without any tea), for there was a large Rolls-Royce of powder-blue awaiting him. It was Esme's dream of unequalled bliss, a dream nourished since the nursery, that one day he might be rich enough to buy and travel (Please hurry up, Perks: her ladyship's train is due) in a powder-blue Rolls-Royce. It was a splendid omen. He sat in front with the chauffeur, right on the edge of his seat, and quivered with excitement.

'How many cars has Mrs Fairweather got?' he enquired.

'Five,' said the chauffeur, 'if you count the garden van and the farm brake.'

Esme was fully prepared to count both.

'But what are the other two?'

'Cadillac and Austin. The Austin's hanging off the railings in the park.'

'How did it get there?'

' 'Er Majesty put it there,' said the chauffeur grimly.

'How?'

'Because she didn't look what she was doing. That's how.'

'Does she often have accidents?'

'More often than not. She'll drive a good car on to the scrap heap in less time than she'll get into bed. Round the corners at fifty with the tyres shrieking – then it's, "Why ain't these tyres been attended to, Simpson, what do you suppose I pay you for?" '

'Have you been with Her Maj— have you been with Mrs Fairweather long?'

'Two weeks,' said the man desperately, 'and not a day too long. Morning, noon and night, "Why, why, why?" "I've driven for twenty years," she says, "and never an accident yet. And now you don't have them tyres blown up and I'm all strung up in the railings." And her doing sixty in the Park. In jug, that's where she'd be by rights, and wouldn't I love to take my notice to 'er there? "Leaving, Simpson?" she says, "Already?" she says, "It's like this, ma'am," I says, "if I stay a week longer, I'll be straight out of 'ere into an 'ome." "You're just like all the rest," she says, "afraid of work and that's the size of it." I'll tell you, sir, she 'asn't kept a man nor a woman for a straight month in fifteen years, what with 'er nagging and 'er nerves and 'er 'ealth and 'er 'usbands – that's it now, sir, ten o'clock from the near-side lamp.'

Esme saw they had turned up a long gravel drive, on either side of which were fields of young corn. The drive was descending slightly, and he saw that it turned left behind a clump of trees after another two hundred yards. The house was visible to the left of the trees, Georgian it seemed in the distance, and surmounted by an entertaining cupola which contained a four-faced clock. The two faces he could see were in aggressive disagreement.

They turned behind the trees and drove into a little courtyard formed by one side of the house (to their right), a sort of kitchen annexe in front of them, and, on the left, a large garage, obviously a converted coach-house. The garage was decorated by a pigeon-cote, so that the whole court was filled with the slow cooing and clumsy fluttering of the birds – a sound too often drowned, as Esme later discovered, by the hysteria of last-minute departures.

The chauffeur whisked him through the open front door and left him in a long, low drawing-room, every corner of which was crowded with vases of beautifully grouped flowers. On either side of the French windows, which opened on to a walled rose garden, were hung two enchanting and unusual Renoirs, while to offset these views of fairyland a magnificent Dégas of a girl at work with an iron was hanging on the far wall. The hunched figure seemed to ignore and yet to dominate the entire room, to gather it together, as though she held in her teeth threads that branched out to every part and object of it.

'*There* you are,' said a voice. It was not quite so formidable as over the wire, it had shrunk, as it were, till it merely belonged to an energetic but unimportant member of the Women's Services. Mrs Fairweather was clutching a dachshund puppy and was soaking wet.

'Fell into the carp-pond,' she said, 'the puppy that is, too young to join the carp, I felt, and McTavish was too busy thinking about his suit to go in himself. Always the same, you see, everything left to me. Come and talk while I bath.'

They went upstairs to a bathroom that was crammed with photos of everything from Royalty as naval cadets to Mrs Fairweather dressed as a coster. Esme politely placed himself just inside her bedroom.

'That's better,' she said, sending her clothes hurtling past him and flinging herself into the bath. 'Now then – Terence – it's him you've come about? Good. McTavish thinks he knows everything, so I'll get my bit in first. Lock the door or that niece of mine will poke her silly face in.'

Esme walked stiffly through the bathroom and locked the door.

'O-o-h-kay then,' she said as he returned to his station in the bedroom, 'well, there's two of them, Terence and Bellamy, good Scottish families – by-blows. Bellamy's all right, plain and good like rice-pudding, happy at Eton, fond of cricket.'

Then a look of regret came into her face. It had once been quite a pretty face – still was perhaps – but soap and water revealed it as white and worn, and under her eyes where she had dolloped heavy mascara patches there remained two lined and rather ludicrous pale-blue crescents.

'It's Terence who gives the trouble,' she said, 'I can't even have them together now. He had to leave Eton – McTavish will tell you – so I sent him to Switzerland. He charms all the analysts and he charms me – then we find him beating the gardener's boy. Then he's mad about America, comics and uniforms and gangs – sent there in the war, my fault as usual I suppose. If he wants a thing he takes it – or orders it, which is worse, and round comes a motor-bike on approval. No real rows yet, thank God, but it's not for the want of trying. He got a lot of guns from Americans near here – kept them in his play-box, tommy-guns and Lügers. A good job I know the local policeman, that's all. It was just perfect heaven when the Commandant found out.'

She dried her hands, and took a cigarette from a box on a wall-bracket.

'Match please – thanks. . . . And then he always has money. Eight Swiss francs a week he's given, yet never has less than thirty they say. Tells the analyst in Zürich he's hungry – "Poor little boy, give him five francs" – down on my bill, of course. Borrows it too, I suppose – but he also takes things from here and sells them there, which is so sweet-natured.

'But he's so adorable sometimes that I pour out money to get him well. Two thousand pounds to psychiatrists last year alone. Then these tutors come, and they're pompous or pansy or they have to work three hours a day, and all say how charming he is while he's busy stealing my camera.'

Had Esme known Mrs Fairweather better, he would have been

24

surprised that she had stuck so long and, by comparison, so coherently to one subject. As it was he felt confused by this mass of inconsequent and ill-expressed detail.

'How old?' he asked.

'Sixteen in September. Wants to go to college in America, but just let him set foot there again and he's had everything as far as I'm concerned. Little rat! Selfish, that's what it is, charming while he has what he wants, but just cross him over one little thing and he'll pull the nearest living creature to bits.'

She began to get out, and Esme hurriedly handed a towel through the door.

'Thanks. You seem to have some manners. And that's another thing: those damned cosmopolitan children, Argentines, Italians, the Lord knows what – they're all with him in Switzerland – have the most diabolical manners you ever saw.'

Esme noticed her language was becoming less clipped: she seemed more at ease, and her conversation was almost literary by contrast with what it had been.

'His table-manners, for instance – the Borgia court on a bank holiday. You have to yell for the salt like a sergeant-major. And if you tick him off he gets moody and goes upstairs to sulk with his precious comic-papers.'

'Boys that age are often a little awkward,' said Esme.

'But you follow up after an hour and find he's bitten the curtains to bits. Jokey, eh?'

'Does he get on with his brother?'

'There you are again. He's madly jealous because his brother's been left in full enjoyment of all the things he affects to despise – Eton and English friends, you know what I mean – and whenever they're together now it's sheer pandemonium. I took Bellamy to Switzerland for Christmas – along with a trained nurse I said was for me (been rather ill lately). We picked up Terence – and within ten minutes he'd bitten Bellamy's left calf till it bled. The nurse was told to take notes on what he said and did, and got enough on paper for a novel.'

'Perhaps he doesn't like being watched.'

'But how did he know? I told him the nurse was interested in Alpine botany. I'm pretty crafty, I can tell you, after three years of this sort of behaviour. We had to have male nurses in London once – told him they were extra waiters for Bellamy's birthday party. Pity we only asked four people, though, there's no getting past him with any old thing.'

Esme said Terence sounded very intelligent; and they went downstairs to see Dr McTavish.

Dr James Andrew McTavish was a socialite psychiatrist and very much on the make. At first sight he was a youngish young man, with an ineffective moustache and the sort of suit you see about on dummies or assistants at the smarter department stores. When he opened his mouth you heard a more or less Scottish accent, and when he shut it you heard the clicking of more or less false teeth; and if he had just preserved his waistline, he had not preserved his hair. While he was shrewd enough to know that he was on to a good thing in psychology, and intelligent enough to make his diagnoses sound plausible, he was also fool enough to take them seriously himself, so that self-satisfaction exuded from every word he spoke. One of the very fluid crowd that formed Mrs Fairweather's junior menagerie of medicos (the senior group, consisting of one semi-defunct but knighted Mayair physician and one obscure Rumanian of vulgar origin, was apparently more or less stable) he was at the moment high enough in favour to be asked for the week-end. For it so happened that the Royal Route to Mrs Fairweather's esteem was to provide a diagnosis even more gruesome and bizarre than the last, and this, on the strength of a recent visit to Switzerland, he had been able to accomplish. A single use of the word paranoia, a term which Mrs Fairweather treated with almost religious reverence, would have kept him in and out of the house for a month, and at fees of his own choosing : but then he considered it necessary to apply a conscientious coating of science to his fictions before producing them as diagnoses. Science and all, however, he had hit on a winner this time.

Esme, watching him sit with the ends of his fingers pressed pretentiously together, surmised that one tribute – however artificial – to the power of the modern substitute for astrology would have McTavish and Mrs Fairweather neatly in the bag.

'Terence Fox's illness,' began the doctor, 'is by no means uncommon and very often curable – provided we get hold of it early enough. It is a type of anti-social neurosis, and frequently takes sadistic forms. This *anti-social tendency*' (the more commonplace the phrase the more significance he strove to lend it) 'was of course intensified when he was compelled to leave Eton College.' (The last two words earned themselves a succulent reverence.) 'While he has yet to do anything criminal, *in the common sense of the word*, his life since then has abounded in acts of what may best be called minor revolt against the social group which has thus rebuffed him. Some of these acts are merely irresponsible, others have a more *stringent* and sadistic tinge (Mrs Fairweather has perhaps told you of what occurred to the gardener's boy). Do you think you can follow my line of thought?'

'I remember,' said Esme, 'in the Army that a man in my platoon was said to be similarly afflicted. In consequence he had become what's known as a prostitute bouncer (if somebody wouldn't pay up, he cut his throat as he went down the stairs). I well remember that we were almost helpless until a detailed psychological analysis had been made: with this very valuable assistance –'

'Exactly,' said McTavish, with a hint of a purr, 'you seem to have followed me well enough to give a legitimate, if rather ominous, parallel. You can imagine then, from your own experience, how worried Mrs Fairweather must be.' Here he gave a deferential nod in her direction. 'But of course,' he continued, 'there are other factors. The boy is extremely intelligent,' (he would be) 'has definite artistic leanings,' (of course) 'and is full of excellent impulses.' (Five guineas worth of encomium.) 'But all this runs the risk of being *vitiated*, perhaps even totally *atrophied*, inasmuch as most of his present energy is diverted into anti-social channels, is used, that is to say, for acts like those of which you have heard or others of petty destruction; while at the same time he is obsessed by representations of violence in ephemeral and pictorial literature. . . . We are at present taking what steps we can, and have hopes of a complete cure,' (a glance at the Dégas) 'if a remote one. Should you be willing to accept the position of tutor, your job, though interesting, would be negative rather than constructive. You would have to observe and report on the boy, above all to see that he does not weaken his position any further by acts that might do him serious – and public – discredit. Do I make myself plain?'

'May one ask,' said Esme, 'why he had to leave Eton? It might give some sort of an idea what to look out for.'

'I was coming to that. It seems he was head of a kind of gang which specialized in picking on sensitive boys and – how shall I put it? – *humiliating* them. He would then name a price of ten shillings or a pound to stop this procedure. Once the money was received,' he continued regretfully, 'the compact was usually forgotten.'

'Oh.'

'What we have got to do is to keep him constantly and beneficially occupied – in company. If left to his own devices, he will disappear without warning and return with disaster in his wake. Drawing and literary activity are valuable as a means of expression, but his products are apt to be distasteful – athletic pastimes are more reliable.

'Indeed,' said Dr McTavish, leaning forward with immense self-satisfaction, 'I have a *hunch*. Sailing,' he said, as though he had just discovered a new element. 'This will be something new, something adventurous, something that demands both attention and discipline. Should there be any practical difficulties, I know of a friend at Aldeburgh who would be prepared to hire out his yacht for a few guineas a week and also to act as guide and instructor. The river Alde, ha! ha!, has its own sense of humour. The town of course is apt to be very crowded in the summer, but I know of a private hotel (run by a cousin of mine) where the food is excellent and all the guests are treated as members of the family.' (Ugh.) 'Do you know anything about sailing, Mr Sa Foy?'

'I can manage small boats,' lied Esme, and mentally reviewed the untold dreariness of all the people he knew who were keen on yachting.

'Good. Well then' – another deferential nod at Mrs Fairweather – 'that can be borne in mind. And then again, tennis, while you are here, is an exc—'

'Am I to be kept on my feet all day, Sandra,' said a husky voice, 'while you finick about in conclave?'

A tall, distinguished man, with grey hair, a guard's tie and a stick on which he was leaning rather heavily, had come in through the French windows.

'Of course not, darling,' said Mrs Fairweather; 'this is Mr Sa Foy who's come to talk about Terence and have dinner. This is Colonel Heffer, Mr Sa Foy. Now you sit down, Ronnie, and talk to Dr McTavish – he's very interested in sailing just now. And I'll take Mr Sa Foy round the garden to meet Tom and Cherry.'

'It's an open question,' said the Colonel, 'whether I'm more bored by sailing or by psychology.'

McTavish gave a 'not long for this world' sort of simper.

'Please don't be childish, Ronnie. Dr McTavish will mix you a drink.'

'I'm not sure,' said McTavish with silky spite, 'that, in his condition, the Col—'

'You will oblige me,' said the Colonel, 'by fetching the brandy and leaving doubts to the inmates of theological colleges. I hope,' he said to Esme, 'that you're not at a theological college?'

'No,' said Esme, 'it's not quite the thing now if you've been at a reasonable school.'

'I've noticed,' said the Colonel, 'that most parsons speak with an accent. What was wrong with being ordained straight from a decent establishment?'

'They felt people should have time to think seriously about vocation.'

'Fancy that,' said Mrs Fairweather, 'I thought people only went into the Church if they were younger sons and too poor for the Army.'

'That's just the point,' said Esme : 'it was thought to be rather irreverent of them. So now they have two years of mortification in a theological college first, to make quite sure they're not just in it for the cash. You have to be very determined to get through.'

'But there's very little cash when you do get through,' said the Colonel.

'Well there you are. Longer and longer preparation for a lower and lower income. It insures sincerity, I'm told.'

'But those accents,' said the Colonel, 'can one never have jobs done these days except by sincere people with accents?' McTavish winced.

'Come along, Mr Sa Foy,' said Mrs Fairweather hurriedly, 'and don't talk too much, Ronnie darling, you mustn't get overtired. You'll see he doesn't, won't you, Dr McTavish?'

But the chances of prolonged conversation between the two of them were small. Esme was swept off into the garden.

'Come back quickly,' called the Colonel, 'I want Mr Sa Foy to tell me about a few more modern fads – like psychoanalysis,' he said with a chuckle.

'The Colonel seems to have taken a fancy to you,' said Mrs

29

Fairweather. They turned out of the rose-garden through a tracery gate in the wall, and walked across a large and beautiful lawn, with exquisitely coloured borders on either side.

'How perfectly lovely,' said Esme – his first sincere and unsolicited comment since his arrival.

'Do you think so? And what do you feel about McTavish?' It was an awkward trick of Mrs Fairweather's to demand the opinions of absolute strangers on anyone from her newest scullery maid to her most habitual hanger-on. The answers invariably gave offence to someone or other: but in this case Esme had the sense to stick to Dr McTavish in his professional capacity.

'He seems to have given a lot of thought to your son.'

'Yes, but of course he can't be expected to have the intuition of a mother who's known a child all its life.' After all, she had filed every letter or report her paid underlings submitted. 'I mean to say, it's not McTavish that has washed his nappies and fed him at his breast – you know what I mean.'

It might just as well have been, thought Esme, for all the suck Mrs Fairweather had ever given.

They were interrupted by the appearance of an unattractive couple who were introduced as 'my cousins, the Valleys'. Mr Valley, it turned out, who had a parody of a moustache and a war record so utterly undistinguished that he still used R.A.F. slang, was 'something' (more or less cultural) in the B.B.C: Mrs Valley being simply a bloody nuisance wherever she set foot, though there was desultory talk of dress-designing. Their real occupation was prancing round Mrs Fairweather to see what they could get – which, to do her justice, was very little in cash, but an overdraft of confidence. The method of insinuation they employed was to let Tom suggest a grievance (against somebody who actually was getting something) and to leave Cherry to work it up. This she did very successfully by sitting on Mrs Fairweather's bed from ten o'clock in the morning – when the poor woman was still so fuddled with methol she could hardly open her eyes – and hypnotizing her into a state of neurotic fury by the unceasing repetition of soft-voiced confidences ('actually smokes in bed and puts the ends in the commode'). It would all end in Mrs Fairweather sweeping downstairs (like an agitated bawdy housekeeper who finds one of her clients has made an unusual request) and clearing some unoffending servant into the street. The Valleys, on the strength of having thus led to the weeding-out of corruption, would then ask to borrow the car for the week-end and disappear in a blaze of vicarious splendour to a Motor Congress : for they had many friends among the motor-racing set, which comprises possibly the nastiest people in the world.

All this, however, was mere background activity. As their objects in life were interference and ingratiation, the best scope of all was afforded by Mrs Fairweather's two sons. Scope for interference, because the boys could be reported on, for ingratiation, because in the case of the elder the reports would usually concern some new and sinister trend in his development which would otherwise have gone unobserved. Presumably then the Valleys deserved thanks on the ground that their observations provided data for a cure, though in fact needless to say they had complicated it beyond measure and materially contributed to its date of completion receding. It followed, however, that the arrival of a new tutor was an important event to them both, for not only would his personal conduct give opportunity for interference, but the possibility of his aggravating some undesirable tendency of Terence's might assist them to earn substantial gratitude. Esme was therefore put firmly, as it were, under the arc-lamp of their discernment, a telling instrument, for it was maintained by the driving power of avarice. Two pairs of eyes assessed his clothes, his hair, his features and his manner; two pairs of ears strained after every intonation of his voice; and two minds decided that he was just the irresponsible trifler necessary to provide occasion for discredit, interference and ingratiation of every kind. A totally admirable choice in fact.

'How wonderful the garden's looking,' said Mrs Valley.

'Don't know how you do it,' said her husband.

'What do you think, Mr Sa Foy?' said Mrs Valley.

'I think it's miraculous,' said Esme.

'Well it's really Sandra's hard work,' she replied.

It was certainly Mrs Fairweather's pride and joy, but she had her moments of fairness.

'The poor man does a great deal,' she murmured.

'I know, Sandra darling, but without your instructions . . .'

'Is Terence interested in gardens?' asked Esme.

'No,' said the Valleys in concert. It was a way of urging his ingratitude.

'Pity,' said Esme, 'with all this. . . .'

'A pity indeed,' said Mrs Valley as snappily as the Queen of Hearts, 'but then so are a lot of things.'

She was a small woman with stumpy legs and a bitchy way of moving. Esme wondered why anyone had ever married her. But she seemed to take her husband for granted – and everything else :

'Come on,' she said greedily, 'we'll go and have a drink.'

A mental review of the situation told Esme that good luck had so far enabled him to play up satisfactorily to everyone present. The Valleys – he couldn't quite see why – seemed to regard him with approval, while the Colonel had conspicuously sought his company and conversation when they were having drinks. More important, Mrs Fairweather seemed to like his manners and the socialite psychiatrist seemed to like his views on psychiatry. All that was needed now, he felt, was a suitable display of ease, together with a becoming diffidence, at the dinner-table. He was therefore very careful not to accept more than three large gins beforehand.

The dining-room gave a subaqueous impression (it was low, rather dark, and surrounded with seascapes), and it was difficult to resist the idea that one was in a party of aquarium exhibits. For once inside the room it was everybody's piscine qualities that predominated. McTavish became slimier than ever, while the habitual ('we are the poor relations but rather well bred') look of gloom on the Valleys was transformed into the snub-nosed stupidity of the turtle – one even forgot the urge to kick them. As for Mrs Fairweather she dashed hither and thither in her zeal to hasten and supplement the efforts of the servants, till she became like one of those tiny, glancing fish with a red streak, that dart from one end of their tanks to the other with insistent and heart-breaking futility. Only the Colonel, whose blood, for all his recent illness, was primed with forty years' worth of excellent claret and salacious stories, still seemed properly to belong to the world of light. He was placed on one side of Mrs Fairweather, Esme on the other. On Esme's left was the psychiatrist, and to his left again was Mr Valley, at the end of the table and thus opposite his hostess; while Mrs Valley was between her husband and the Colonel.

'. . . But she should never have gone to that house,' Mrs Fairweather was saying. 'Eddie Chynnon thought he'd get in well with the Brummels by lending his house for the wedding breakfast, but *she* was under no compulsion to attend it, even if the bridegroom was her godson. For one thing, Eddie's extremely vulgar, and for another, he made a lot of money out of his wife which he's now busy spending on m— on other people,' she concluded lamely.

McTavish had his line in social chit-chat, it appeared.

'It's said,' he contributed, 'that she was *specifically* warned of all the circumstances, but merely said, "There has yet to be a scene at a wedding breakfast."'

'She must have forgotten a good deal,' said Mrs Fairweather.

'Well, there you are. I know she said that, because the lady's maid is sent to me for treatment – she picks the spots on her face in order to draw attention to herself. Unfortunately she developed piles and started –'

'But I do agree, Sandra,' said Mrs Valley quickly, 'you've known *her* so long – before she was married too – and you understand her so well. Couldn't you have . . . ?'

'We all did our best,' said Mrs Fairweather, 'but I've always said there are three races of mankind – Blacks, Whites and *them* – once they get an idea, they've got it – the Bourbon thing,' she added vaguely.

By this time the second course was on the table. Esme was discovering, too late, that Mrs Fairweather's gin was nothing if not diuretic. He must stick to his post, to leave the room would be fatal. . . .

'How do you like the claret, Mr Sa Foy?' his hostess asked.

'Excellent,' said Esme, pulling himself together, 'but am I right in saying that another two years will see it past its best?'

'Yes,' she said with a look of appraisal, 'it's a Conton '26 and we've no time to lose with it. I'm working it off on all my friends – I shall hope to work some of it off on you.' Better and better.

'I should be delighted,' said Esme modestly. One thing about claret, he thought gloomily, it was less insistent than gin.

Mr Valley took the opportunity for vicarious ingratiation.

'Must be awfully interesting,' he said to McTavish, 'meeting important people and finding out what's underneath it all.'

'Piles?' said the Colonel, helping himself to claret. Mrs Fairweather, off on an excursion to the kitchen, tripped over the bell-wire. McTavish simpered.

The silence was abysmal. Now, if ever, was the time to exhibit social deftness.

'I'm told the celebrations for the Fourth of June went very well,' said Esme. After all, *one* of Mrs Fairweather's sons was still safely installed at Eton.

'Who told you that?' said Mrs Valley fiercely.

'A friend of mine who was there – Reresby Lyewell,' said Esme.

'Oh, those Lyewells,' said Mrs Fairweather, prancing back into the room, 'and how do you come to know Reresby?'

'He was up at Cambridge for a year with me.'

'Ah,' she said voraciously, 'at last I've found someone who knew him there. Will you please, please tell me, why did he go down so suddenly? His uncle talks such nonsense. . . .'

The story was long and amusing, and Esme did it justice. With a sigh of relief and a sense of having saved the situation he went into the well-rehearsed routine of Reresby's outrageous waistcoats and still more outrageous parties, his well-known collection of rare snuffs and his equally well-known collection of fêted but faithless mistresses, the dust gathering on his books and the bills gathering on his desk, and the inevitable culmination in failure, disaster and debt. It was the kind of story people are never tired of hearing about the sons and nephews of their acquaintances. It was told with vigour and received with rapture – and sent Mrs Fairweather off on a seemingly interminable series of reminiscences about the meanness of Reresby's uncle and the shifts to which this quality had reduced his aunt.

'And at the big Lyewell parties before the war,' she rattled on, 'there was only one subject of conversation, when would the orangeade run out? So that when the buffet started there was a cataclysmic rush and . . .'

On she went and on. Esme was getting desperate. He had by now extracted a severe wince of pain from McTavish and had come near to kicking Mrs Fairweather herself. He was hanging on (quite literally) like grim death.

But he was saved by the gong. Just as Sir George Lyewell had developed his third pair of horns, rounds of frantic abuse were heard outside, which turned out to be the chauffeur and the cook quarrelling about the last bottle of beer in the pantry. Mrs Fairweather and her niece went to umpire, and the men retired. Esme felt he had given a very good account of himself.

34

So, on the whole, did Mrs Fairweather. His looks and his manners had started him off with a substantial credit. Added to this, he had listened with attention and apparent intelligence when she was telling him about Terence – he had even behaved respectfully to McTavish, which was unusual among her acquaintance. Then he had been excellent with the Colonel and rather amusing at dinner – though she was inclined to wonder whether his story about Reresby Lyewell hadn't rather a dubious moral tone. In fact now she thought of it, Esme looked as if he had rather a dubious moral tone all round. Still, the reference from his college was excellent, it seemed he had done well in his examinations, and in any case it would be a change to have someone around – not that she'd see that much of him – whose general pleasantness was beyond dispute. On the whole it was a promising outlook, she felt – as indeed she had felt about a number of men, in various capacities and with the same ultimately disastrous result, during the past twenty-five years.

By the time she had seen to the cook, the chauffeur, and her face, Esme was radiant with relief and brandy. She swept him off into the library to discuss terms; and as usual started off with a topic as far as possible removed from the one with which she was really concerned. (This explained why it took her five times as long as anyone else to transact the most elementary piece of business : she always got bogged down over introductory trivialities.)

'How do you think the Colonel looks?' she asked.

'A little pale,' said Esme, 'but most distinguished.'

'He's been given three weeks, I'm afraid – they felt he might just as well enjoy himself down here as eat his heart out in hospital. He might die in the night, and really, though it would be so upsetting for me, it might be a blessed relief. He's been so used to a life of activity and pleasure. We took him to Epsom the other day, and some dreadful creature said, "There's poor Ronnie Heffer – he'll soon be butcher's meat," in a voice like a fog-horn, so now he knows, but he's wonderfully brave.'

'I thought him enchanting.'

'He is – and he thinks you're so nice. So do I too, the moment I saw you I said, "He's just the one" – but now we must talk dates – and terms.' Her face hardened perceptibly. 'Well, I shall want you to join me on the afternoon of the fifth – Terence flies back that day, little American maniac – can you manage that?

35

It's 6, St Ambrose Gate, the London address, 'phone Victoria 7888
– my private number, it's a deadly secret.

'Now terms,' she said.

Esme giggled. 'I'm afraid I'm very bad at this side of it all.'

'So am I' – she giggled too.

'Liar,' they both thought.

'Well as a rule seven pounds a week – with all found, is the
thing.'

'But in this case,' said Esme, with drunken courage of the sort
which wins V.C.s, 'the circumstances, I think you'll agree, warrant
a slight increase – three pounds a week, let us say, which will give
us a round figure. I mean, there is this question of *never* leaving
him, the additional trouble a boy of his type, though artistic and
interesting, is liable to cause, even perhaps a slight personal risk.
. . . Then there is the danger of *public* . . . you see what I mean?'

She did. 'Very well,' she said, with an effort at charm and the
look of a gorgon : 'but of course you'll have no other calls on your
time? Work for exams or anything?'

'I shall be entirely at your disposal,' replied Esme.

Going home, after a drink or two with the chauffeur while waiting for the train, Esme thought to himself that this was what came
of extravagance. A room with a bathroom, she had said, ten quid
a week, all found, and the Conton '26. She had also talked of the
Continent. The boy, they said, must be guided, and his taste
improved to fit his position. If only, thought Esme, he could be
guided into congenial channels, his tastes could be brought into a
scope that would suit his position as much as they would befit his
mother's income.

# III

The Honourable Mrs Sandra Fairweather, as her friends used to say, had been born a Fox and had remained, despite marriage, a vixen. Now the Foxes were a very reputable family with a country house and a penchant for Royalty of all sorts and sizes. They were also extremely well-to-do (Mrs Fairweather's grandfather had been an extensive slum-landlord), and although Sandra was the only girl and had four elder brothers, it was early made clear to her that she could expect a considerable fortune, conditional only on reasonable behaviour. It was perhaps the constant repetition throughout her childhood of this condition which explained why her whole life was a battleground in which sexiness was always, apparently, just worsted in the struggle with propriety. Others again explained this phenomenon by pointing to the shock she must have received when her youngest brother was the victim of an incident in the conservatory which involved a Cabinet Minister – an affair which caused old Mrs Fox to create such a hue and cry that the Minister finally shot himself. It was silly of Mrs Fox : for the boy, as a result, was never the same again (his mother, with a typical mixture of moral indignation and vanity, never let him forget he had helped to cause the suicide of a Minister of the Crown), and spent the rest of his life writing indifferent novels about Cabinet Ministers, presumably in the hope that twenty fictitious creatures of his pen would be taken, on the Day of Judgment, to atone for one creation of God. Sandra also, the rumour went, was rather shaken by this occurrence; but whether this was due merely to consanguinity, or to the possible fact that she too liked romping in the conservatory with Cabinet Ministers, was never explained.

At school (a convent) she did rather well, for in a slapdash way she was an intelligent child, and always retained a genuine love of literature, which was to yield harvest, later on, in the form of delicate, tenuous, and privately-printed books of not intolerable poetry. But what caused considerably more satisfaction was that she was growing up to be remarkably beautiful. When she was twenty it was whispered that she could have any hand in the realm; for apart from her beauty, the neurotic instability that was already becoming apparent, far from proving an impediment, was socially manifested by fearlessness in the hunting field, a swift and inconsequent humour at the dinner-table, and the ability to cause excitement, even on a Sunday afternoon, either by losing her jewels or baiting her chaperon.

For three years, however, she hung fire. People began to say (nor were they wrong) that neurosis, when combined with youth, could be a social asset for a few years but would become a matrimonial liability in a few days. Then, without warning, a young man called Faunus de Wett, who belonged to a well-known racing family and was as rich and pampered as herself, became engaged and married to her within two short months. The marriage took place at St Peter's, Eaton Square : much champagne was drunk, and while many tongues were temporarily silenced, as many heads were vigorously shaken.

Old Mrs Fox lived just long enough to tell everyone how radiantly happy they were (they never came near her, since she was by now as boring as she was blind) : and then passed serenely away, in time to be spared the next instalment. For once she was out of the way, trouble set in with a vengeance. Faunus was a pleasant enough young man, and was even making sincere efforts, since he understood his wife was a woman of culture, to speak, once in a fortnight, of something other than racehorses. (His wedding gift to his bride had been a noble string of two-year-olds.) Sandra, on the other hand (as had been confidently predicted), was making no effort whatever to adapt herself to Faunus. She was swiftly developing a taste for trans-Continental travel; and had a happy knack of devising trips that started on the day of the Two Thousand and finished a week later than the St Leger. On the second of these Faunus refused to accompany her. It was too much, he said. Indeed it was, she replied; and he was to remember she had money of her own and was quite prepared to show a little independence. Well then, good riddance.

But there was still hope for the marriage. A month later she returned with the news that Faunus might expect an heir. He was a generous youth and sincerely touched. For the next few months he abandoned everything and devoted himself solely to keeping her happy and in good health. Then the child was born – lamentably but unambiguously dead.

It was this which turned Sandra finally sour. She was to have her days of happiness in the future – there were even to be days when she gave a little : but she had conceived a grudge against the male sex which never lay long beneath the surface and which, combined with an aggravation of her already dangerous tendency to live off her nerves and not her daily bread, made life for her immediate entourage an affair that would have crushed a Titan. Faunus was blamed for everything, from the loss of the child to the loss of the *Sunday Times*. Faunus was selfish, indifferent and wicked. Faunus was a wretch and Faunus must go – divorced, as became a gentleman, by her. Gladly, he cried in response; he would give any amount of money, he would confess publicly to any shame she might decree; he would change his life, his principles, his name, and, were it possible, his sex – if only he might be free. And free, after a year of lawyer's letters and the payment to Sandra (Anything ! Anything !) of half his considerable fortune – free, at last, he became – only to be granted, six months later, the broader freedom of death.

After the excitement, Sandra decided on a holiday in America. She took a large house on Long Island and entertained female columnists. She had a swimming-pool put in and entertained male film stars. One day someone handed a female columnist a cheque, and Sandra found herself entertaining Earl Marshal Acre, Junior, a prematurely bald young man without any eyebrows, who was third in line to a Dublin innkeeper and immediate heir to a rolling-stock fortune. He had heard that the Duke of Panton had looked favourably on Sandra and was prepared, having seen her in the distance, to do the same himself.

Oddly enough, though both character and masculinity were barely perceptible in him, Sandra was prepared to look favourably back. After they had met he came often to Long Island, where he spent days of delirious happiness in fetching and carrying for a woman of whom the Duke of Panton had approved. He listened with sympathy and a hundred times to the tale of the iniquitous Faunus. He wept when a favourite dachshund died. He approved each new and promising footman as he appeared and heaped indignation on the ungrateful wretch when he gave notice. He swam in the swimming-pool, revealing spindly legs and an atrocious figure. But Sandra barely noticed either. She wanted a man on a string whose admiration was unqualified and whose sympathy was bottomless. She now had one. And odd though it may seem, Earl Marshal Acre, Junior, was by this time, Duke or no Duke, genuinely and passionately in love. His passion was really the only proof of his existence : apart from an affection for money – which to do him justice was weaker than in many of his kind – it was the only positive emotion he had ever felt, the first – and the last.

For they decided to spend the honeymoon in California, by themselves and at an unfashionable time of the year. Three weeks after it began Earl Marshal Acre was found dead in a downstairs cloakroom, having shot himself through the head. He left no explanation, only an apology for the venue he had chosen, which, he said, was unavoidable, as he did not wish to alarm his wife by being found dead in their bedroom. That California is prolific in open spaces had not, apparently, occurred to him.

Although the rolling-stock fortune was still in the hands of his father, he had been given, on attaining his majority, a considerable sum of his own. So Sandra departed to Europe, bewildered and rather hurt, and richer by the equivalent of half a million sterling. The matter of Acre's suicide remained obscure. Even Sandra, it was said, had not had time to madden him. He was rich, he was newly and, in supposition at least, very happily married. He had no debts, and he was due to become richer. The thinness of his blood and the timidity of his nature precluded the possibility of the sort of scandal that brings blackmail. Motive there was none; and had it not been for his own note of confession, foul play would have been suspected. As it was, the papers were bribed into maintaining comparative silence, while even his nearest friends remained, from that day forth, in complete mystification. Or so it was always said.

For two years no one heard much of Sandra. Then she bought herself a large house in a fashionable district of London and appeared with a baby boy of about one year old, whom she had adopted, she said, and given her maiden name. Six months later she announced her intention of adopting another child, did so, and purchased for their upbringing another large house in a most unhealthy fen district. But both boys had been begotten by young parents who had enjoyed the process. They were strong and beautiful, and flourished, despite the fen air and an almost weekly change of nurses, like the two young princes of a fairy tale.

But having once got them, Sandra, apart from unsuccessfully soliciting Royal godparents, then forgot them. Gradually the nurses changed less often, until, finally, save for the unexpected and catastrophic fenland week-ends that Sandra periodically undertook (the boredom of which compelled her to sack somebody) they remained almost constant. She rushed hectically from Paris to New York and then back again to Cannes and even, on occasion, to London : and when she thought of her adopted sons at all, it was only to assure herself that the affection they owed her, in return for such self-sacrifice, was immense if not infinite. They, meanwhile, played happily enough at Badlock, occasionally went to London to be bought new clothes, and remained entirely indifferent to the beautiful and excitable woman to whom they wrote once in a week and saw twice in a twelvemonth. Then in 1939 came the war, the fenland house was shut up, and they were hastily dispatched to America where they remained for the next six years.

As for Sandra, she had a whale of a war at the Savoy, and concluded it by marrying for the third time. She began by being something in the Red Cross, a position which, as she saw it, called for twice the number of expensive telephone calls that had been requested in the most hysterical hunts for pre-war luggage lost in transit. She, who in her time had sacked and engaged a whole regiment of secretaries over the wire, would surely be a very valuable asset in the Crown's defence. She also specialized in wild-cat schemes of an impromptu nature; and it was during the third and most disastrous of these, on which she was busy with the energy of a herd of elephant and the foresight of a child of two, that she collapsed in a fit of nervous prostration. She was carried to her bedroom, where she stayed for four days in seven during the remainder of the duration, requiring the attentions of half a squad of nurses while she was upstairs and dislocating the organization of an entire Civil Defence District whenever she came down. Towards the end of 1943, comparatively minor losses in part of the slum properties led to her becoming really very ill indeed : and it was during this illness she first met two people who were to loom large in her life for the next few years.

The first was a Rumanian doctor called Fibula Trito, who alone succeeded in persuading her she could recover without the removal of most of her insides. He brought off a brilliant cure and became the most trusted among the effective physicians she employed. It was indeed largely due to her that he later abandoned general practice for the more lucrative realm of psychology. He had had the shrewdness to realize that her illness was vast but largely imaginary, and relied almost entirely on personality for his cure. The success was a surprise to him, but he at once realized that a perpetual smile and complete silence (which had the additional advantage of saving him the effort of speaking English) generated an atmosphere of confidence worth many grains of penicillin. Furthermore the money which would have been spent on penicillin could now be added to his fee. Finally, and best of all, his new technique was best suited to purely mental illnesses : to specialize in these would save the trouble and expense of elaborate equipment, while if such equipment should be really necessary, he could always recommend his clients (for a handsome commission) to colleagues who were also co-religionists.

Sandra's second meeting was with the Hon. Simon Fairweather, who happened to be a very remote cousin on leave in London and at a loose end. He was ten years younger than Sandra, and the last time she had seen him was in the nursery. As the youngest son of the tenth Earl of Plurimum he had been given the job (before the war) of running the family laundry, an occupation which was not so much demanding as merely monotonous and had provoked endless mirth in all his friends, who would send him their shirts to wash and then complain about the loss of imaginary buttons. But he had no money and therefore no alternative : and indeed he only came to see Sandra in the hope that this attention would lead to a remembrance (however slender) in her will, for she had put it about the family that her days in the Savoy were rapidly running out.

Something about this young man, whether his uniform or his obsequiousness, caught Sandra's fancy, so that she asked him to call again. This he did with a good grace and a bunch of expensive flowers. She noticed with approval that he had the same excellence as a sympathetic listener that had characterized poor Marshal Acre. The next time he came on leave he called several times, and Sandra, having by now learned from Trito that she would both live and retain her insides, suddenly asked him to marry her, promised him a large settlement, and said that he would be such a help in bringing up the children. Simon, who was daily expecting arrest for passing three large but worthless cheques, consented with avidity, and they were married the following week by special licence and in her bedroom.

Nor can her motives be said to have been altogether obscure. Here at last was someone who, having neither money to retreat with nor courage to shoot himself, couldn't get away, someone therefore on whom she could vent without interruption the resentment she now harboured against the entire population of grown males. They had treated her shabbily and must now provide a scapegoat. In Simon Fairweather she had a scapegoat with an unexceptionable pedigree, five thousand pounds worth of education, and a genuine if remote chance of inheriting an earldom.

And indeed it seemed she was right. A settlement, she had decided, was unsatisfactory, and Simon was in consequence receiving a handsome but easily withdrawable allowance. Unlike poor Faunus he could not retire into the shelter of his own resources: and he was much too weak-kneed to emulate the motiveless but undeniable courage of Earl Marshal Acre, Junior. Whichever way you looked at it Simon was there for life.

And for the matter of that he did not at first object. But then he still had his freedom. He was stationed in Yorkshire, where he was not indeed safe from Sandra's telephone calls but whither she showed no desire to follow him. If only he had thought a moment, he would have realized she knew a trick worth two of that. For within three months she had done her work; a major-general of her acquaintance had used his influence to place Simon in the War Office – a preferable alternative, the poor man felt, to being driven slowly insane by hourly calls from Sandra at the Savoy. Mrs Sandra Fairweather was once again turning the screw. What was more, she meant to get her money's worth. This was the first time she had had to pay out, she was paying out lucratively (what with the war and the doctors, she could scarcely call two million her own), and Simon must realize his responsibilities –

responsibilities beside which those of his position at the War Office paled to insignificance. The major-general, who was just settling down to a well-earned period of peace, found his troubles had scarcely begun. At any hour he might be called on to give Major Fairweather leave of absence so that he might attend to some whim of his wife's – whims which ranged hilariously from mere dizzy spells to long week-ends in Cornwall. For Mrs Fairweather was now fairly convalescent.

If her convalescence was agony for Simon and the general, her eventual recovery was unmitigated torture. She would even arrive in person at the War Office to sweep the blushing major off to lunch until four o'clock – usually on the pretext that she must discuss with him the war damage sustained by her property, by which she appeared much troubled. By May '45 he knew every word in the title-deeds for the three slum-houses that had suffered.

He also knew another thing. If it meant penury and the family laundry for the rest of his life, if it meant he never wrote another good cheque for as long as he lived, he was going to leave Sandra. Soon he would be demobilized and the last vestige of an excuse for absenting himself would be lost. Whatever happened, he was going.

Nor was he without a certain instinct for self-preservation. He walked out of his wife's house in the autumn of '45, a day later, she noticed bitterly, than his quarterly allowance had reached his bank.

From that day on she turned in desperation to her two sons. For some time now she had been making rather sluggish arrangements to retrieve them. A week after Simon's departure she set out in person for America. The heat, as they say in that country, was on.

Heaven alone knew what she expected to find when she got there, but it certainly included affection. What she actually did find was two very good-looking little boys with American accents, extravagant habits, a complete ignorance of good manners, and a very guarded attitude towards herself. The first three, she decided, needed nothing more than a good preparatory school, the last a good dose of her own company. This latter they could have till Christmas, after which they could be despatched to a suitable school on the south coast. In the meantime she whisked them home

44

in an aeroplane, opened the fenland house, and set about finding the first of many tutors.

It was now her sons' turn to join the swelling crowd of men about whom she had been disillusioned. The younger boy, it was true, was a nice, unintelligent child who tried to do what was expected of him. But the production of love *de vacuo* was beyond his power, the simulation of it alien to his nature. This, however, was not what really bothered Mrs Fairweather. For the younger son's case had at least the compensation that, being essentially British by make-up, he was soon brought to conform in the matters of accent and manners; and added to this, it was not his love she really required.

It was the elder son, Terence Ambrose Fox, just over eleven years of age, who could have been the consolation for all she imagined she had suffered, but who was instead the final point of focus for the long-accumulated misery of her own ill-adjusted nature. He was a fine and handsome child with long, graceful limbs and a beautiful smile : he was intelligent and, for his age, very witty; but he was also selfish, captious and strong-willed, and any love he had was not to be bestowed on a mother he had seldom seen. As for his behaviour, it left much to be desired. He adored anything that came from America – whether clothes, books or firearms – a trait that was not in the least pleasing to his mother, who had had something of a reaction since the time of Marshal Acre. Again, he had all the contempt of the strong for the weak, a tendency which American comic-papers, with their insistence on violence, had considerably aggravated. He was grossly and unrepentantly extravagant. He was extremely lazy where he saw no good cause for using up energy. Indeed the sum of it all was simply and solely that he lacked moral sense : for he had already learnt that charm and intelligence can achieve most things, and he therefore resented being opposed on other grounds which he did not in the least understand.

Sandra threw herself into the battle with all her spasmodic intensity. Habit had, of course, gone too far for her to think of remaining very long in the same place, but her visits to the boys, whether at home or at school, became more frequent and more hysterical than ever. A succession of tutors made the holidays seem like the flickering films of 1920, while the headmaster of their school knew barely a week's peace at a time. She would have crazes for investigating the food, the sanitation, the educational principles employed – anything and everything that might affect the condition of her sons and had the further attraction of being entirely beyond her experience. But while the younger boy, if he got no cleverer, was at least turning into a suitable subject for Eton, the elder remained as cynical and unsatisfactory as ever. He had by now discovered that a show of affection towards his mother was certain to achieve a lavish reward, and his ingenuous manner made such hypocritical build-ups fairly easy to effect : so that the let-downs, by contrast, were becoming increasingly violent and ferocious, and would use up, when they occurred, every shred of emotion in the house.

It was about then that the great deduction was made. Vanity precluded Sandra from believing that her son could be deliberate in his evasion of her possessive advances, nor did it permit her to acknowledge as her son, adopted or not, a boy who was deficient in moral sense. It only remained that he should have something wrong in a psychological way. Dr Trito was summoned and disaster ensued.

For Dr Fibula Trito's post-war practice had not flourished in correspondence with his hopes. In the case of Terence Fox he scented a basic annual income for several years to follow. To this end he made a profound diagnosis, suggested that the intermittent assistance of several other doctors he could recommend would be required, and with skill that can only be admired proceeded to hedge the wretched Terence round at once with suspicion and with sympathy. From now on he was watched and nagged, forbidden very reasonable pleasures and compelled to take others at once duller and more expensive, and subjected, in general, to a petty and appalling regime of immense latitude in some directions and absurd confinement in others. At first the boy was hurt, then he was amused; and finally he determined to exploit the circumstances to the best of his ability. This meant stringing along Trito with occasional relapses in order to prove he still needed attention. For a while all went well. Then in 1948, rather to Terence's annoyance Trito announced that, if Mrs Fairweather would take the responsibility, her son might now be sent to Eton.

But Terence had now been playing this game for a year, and sensed interesting possibilities altogether remote from Windsor. He accordingly did his best to get expelled and had an entertaining time in the process. Meanwhile an agitated house-master prolonged the farce for as long as possible in view of the wealth and position of Mrs Fairweather, the peace of mind of the younger boy (who arrived two halves later), and out of genuine sympathy for what he conceived to be a difficult but not incurable illness of the soul. He was a great one for the Psyche and the two-horsed chariot, and continued to back the loser.

This poor booby's patience was long but not eternal. The incident of what McTavish called 'humiliating' a number of boys had finally set the seal on Terence's Eton career, and one day he appeared in London, fresh and unrepentant from this engaging *jeu d'esprit*, to face a palpitating Sandra (previously warned by telegram) and a very thoughtful Trito, whose secret estimate as to the duration of Terence's stay at Eton had been correct to the nearest two months.

It was now that Sandra well and truly lost her head. With a minimum of negotiation, her name and wealth would have procured Terence instant entry to any public school other than the first six in the land. To be sure the episode would have required a little explanation to her friends; but by sending the boy to Switzerland, where Trito knew of a very suitable instit— or rather school, she finally stamped him 'sacked or supered' for life. Not that he cared, or for that matter, that anyone bothered very much as things run nowadays. But it made one thing very plain – Sandra was losing her grip. From now on her friends settled comfortably down to the spectacle of a decline. Once the doctor had the first say – they all knew the symptoms.

To do Trito justice, Terence was very happy in Switzerland. He made a number of friends of varied nationality, wide interests, precocious intelligence and precarious morals. It was quite possibly the best thing that could have happened to him. But it did not improve his attitude towards Sandra (who was quickly recognized and rationalized as a basically common phenomenon among the parents of the Summit School, near Zürich); and when she arrived to spend Christmas at St Moritz (accompanied by Bellamy, Trito, Mr and Mrs Valley, and a trained nurse with an enormous notebook) the vigorous young hooligan she found awaiting her filled her with every species of frustration and dismay. Nor had things improved by the following April. Still, Trito said that *au fond* the situation was on the mend (an expression he used to cheer his clients up during prolonged periods of atrophy) and, in any case Terence would be spending nine weeks at home in the summer. Steps could be taken then. So it was at this juncture, with the arrival of Terence at Kensington Air Station appointed for 6 p.m. on July 5, just two weeks away, that Esme found himself engaged as private tutor to the eldest adopted son of the Honourable Mrs Sandra Fairweather, *née* Fox.

# IV

It was hardly to be expected that the arrangements for Esme's appearance in London should be left unaltered. Indeed it was a miracle they were only altered once.

The day previously fixed was a Wednesday. On the Monday Esme, who was spending a long and accompanied week-end in a pub at Brighton and had thought he was entirely beyond reach, was astonished to receive a telegram from Mrs Fairweather in which he was asked to ring her private number that night and no matter how late he might come in. It was a salutary general lesson for him that anyone who had a telephone and no regard for expense could trace anyone else in time. (The head-porter of his college had overheard the week-end rendezvous being made; the college was the first place Mrs Fairweather had tried; and the good man's natural discretion had soon been reduced to quavering capitulation.) Esme might also have deduced – as in any case he very soon learnt – that no one was safe from Mrs Fairweather while anything less than the Atlantic Ocean was between them.

There was nothing for it. He rang the number, uncomfortably aware that he was well the worse for drink.

'Mr Sa Foy here,' he said, 'I –'

'Ah,' said a voice like all the furies in concert, 'having a little jaunt in Brighton, eh?'

'Yes,' said Esme.

'Well, I hope you're having fun,' said the voice more malignantly than ever, for Mrs Fairweather resented not knowing where people were even if she had no legitimate claim on them, 'but the thing is this. There's been a telegram from Terence saying he's coming a day early. Meaning tomorrow.'

This, Esme reflected, meant she was laid open to spending

49

twenty-four hours alone with him. By the sound of it all she would prefer a bank holiday on the waters of Acheron. Caught again.

'But of course,' he said, 'if you'd like me to – '

'What about Brighton?' said Mrs Fairweather, who, having gained her point, was always ferociously considerate in retrospect.

'That's quite all right, I assure you. In any case – ' careful, careful, there's capital to be made out of this, ' – I can easily cancel all my engagements. Except lunch on Wednesday, if that's all right.' One must put a price on oneself.

'I suppose so.' Ferocious consideration seldom extended to actual concessions.

'Tomorrow evening at five then? 6, St Ambrose Gate?' said Esme.

'If you please. I think it's perfectly divine of you,' she concluded without sincerity. Esme had made less capital than he might have. As usual he had been too emphatic about his own unselfishness.


He arrived the following afternoon, after a trying scene with the other half of his accompanied week-end, who wanted them to have tea with her mother. This was obviously a grossly inconsiderate request, in view of the nervous strain Esme was under – as he himself pointed out. But it was at least an open question whether the strain hadn't been increased more by the subsequent quarrel than it would have been by a week of having tea with people's mothers.

Mrs Fairweather, with Mrs Valley in attendance, was making flurried preparations for a descent on Kensington Air Station.

'No time for tea, no time for tea,' she kept saying.

'I've had mine,' said Esme sillily.

'Get a look at these,' she replied inconsequently – these being a set of amber beads, 'they're meant to remind me of something.'

'They're delicious, at any rate,' said Esme.

'Sandra has such lovely taste,' said Mrs Valley.

'——' said Sandra, who had laddered a stocking.

Esme, feeling something was expected, teetered about as though he had mended stockings all his life.

'I know,' she said, 'Biarritz.'

Mrs Valley raised her eyebrows.

'Such a heavenly place for children,' Sandra went on, 'it's where those beads came from. I was going to mention it to you – it'd be such fun to go there, and it's just the thing for Terence.'

'I'm sure it's heaven,' said Esme.

'Are you quite certain, darling –' began Mrs Valley.

'Certain of what?'

'About Biarritz being suitable.'

'Of course it's suitable. Charles was almost brought up there.'

'But he's been to prison since.'

'That wasn't Biarritz, it was kleptomania.'

But as usual Mrs Valley had sown the seeds of doubt. Then she turned to Esme.

'Where did you get that suit?' she said, 'my husband's so anxious to find something ready-made.'

'Harrods,' said Esme in a fury.

'Well, I'm not at all sure he'll want to go there. I'll tell him though.'

'Ready, Mr Sa Foy?' asked Sandra, 'we've got ten minutes.'

'I must go home, darling,' said Mrs Valley with a long-suffering look, 'and make poor Tom his supper.'

To his great joy, Esme found they were going in the powder-blue Rolls. There was no sign of the chauffeur (who had gone to seek other employment), and Sandra was going to drive. As they passed Buckingham Palace she discovered it was really only three minutes they had, so they turned down towards the Wellington statue as though all the hounds in Leicestershire were after them. Esme trembled for his beloved Rolls.

At Hyde Park Corner they were engaged in a jam and a Billingsgate match with a taxi-driver. By the Albert Hall they took somebody's indicator off.

'No time,' gasped Sandra through her cigarette : 'take my number,' she yelled, and they zoomed onward.

'Thought we'd go to the cinema tonight,' she said, 'dinner out – the cook's at Badlock. Must be somewhere where I can't *see* Terence, or I'll probably tear him apart.'

'That'll be very nice – the cinema, I mean.'

'Oh, yes, and here's five quid for expenses, meant to give it you before.'

She left the steering-wheel to take care of itself, dug some cash out of her handbag, realized they had overshot the air station by quarter of a mile, turned in the middle of the road without looking, and roared back.

'Take it,' she gasped, drawing up with scrunch just fifteen minutes late.

Terence was waiting inside, smoking a cigarette, chewing gum, and sitting on his trunk. He wore a gaberdine suit and a tie with a parrot on it – or rather a parrot in the shape of a tie. His face was very handsome and rather young for his age, but it wore a sly and sensual sneer, so that it resembled a late Hellenistic statue of Pan. Esme saw that his forehead was small, narrow and indeed criminal; but there was no doubt that his smile, which he turned on for a moment when he saw his mother, was of extraordinary charm and beauty, for it revealed perfect teeth and converted the expression of his lips into an ordinary, good-humoured sensuality instead of the rather sinister concupiscence they had previously indicated. The cigarette disappeared as though he had been a conjuror, but the gum, which he had forgotten, remained.

'Darling,' said Mrs Fairweather, and enveloped him: 'how perfectly lovely to see you – oh take that wretched gum out of your mouth.'

Terence complied and winked at Esme. When they were back in the Rolls he parked it on her shoe as she bent back to reach for something. Esme began to like him. When they reached the Horse Guards' barracks she found her foot stuck to the clutch, wrenched it away in fury, and stalled the engine. There was a crunch behind, and horns blared. Meanwhile Sandra was picking the loathsome mess off her shoe.

'Devil,' she said, turning on Terence. 'Devil.' Then she flung the shoe out of the window to fall at the foot of the astonished sentry. 'That'll come off your birthday present,' she remarked in a frozen voice.

After that they drove home without a word.


Once at St Ambrose Gate, Sandra started to change once more, this time for dinner. Besides which a young Swiss called Monsieur André had appeared to do something to her hair. Regardless of the fact that Terence knew French almost as well as English (a year in Switzerland had at least seen to that) she commenced on a rapid and demotic account for Monsieur André's benefit of the chewing-gum affair. Terence giggled and led Esme off to be shown his American magazines.

These were of three types – comics, science-fiction and horror stories. The comics were relatively educational, being concerned mainly with figures such as Plastic Man or Kid Eternity who devoted their rather equivocal powers to a disagreeable defence of public morality. Science-fiction, on the other hand, was largely amoral : its heroes were androgynous young men in knee-boots and breast-plates, who flitted from end to end of the cosmos, occasionally being blasted with a ray-gun or getting lost in a time-stream. As a boy Esme had had a passion for tales of this type, but they seemed to have developed a great deal since his time, to have lost whatever humanity they had once possessed, and to have been compelled to sacrifice any idea of adventure to an increasing demand for mere pseudo-scientific novelty. Horror stories, finally, were frankly revolting. On the covers green and red monsters either made love or tore each other to bits, while inside there was page after page of bizarre circus antics 'beyond the grave' or in the 'slimy recesses of the Congo'. It puzzled Esme that anyone so apparently intelligent and humorous as Terence should bother about such stuff. The answer was simply that in America it was 'the thing'. Terence would spend hours of fascinated study over these magazines, and then claim that he was merely trying to assess the mental qualities of current American boyhood. This plea had a certain rather dubious ring of authenticity; but what really led Esme to capitulate to the magazines was learning that their main purpose was to be hired out or sold at enormous profit in Terence's Swiss school, there being a dearth of such literature in Switzerland. So it was arranged that next day they should visit a store in St Martin's Lane which abounded in these atrocities, and there lay the foundation of a new and lucrative business against Terence's return in the autumn. Esme thus took the first step along the road to winning the boy's approbation, but he had an uneasy suspicion that Mrs Fairweather would not endorse his method.

The conversation then turned on the house they were in. Esme, still feeling his way, said how nice it was. Terence, almost forget-ting his American accent in his excitement, differed firmly. To be brought to St Ambrose Gate, he pointed out, was always the preliminary to some particularly dastardly move on the part of his mother.

'It's the jumping-off place for the big Shanghai,' he explained : 'when I went to Switzerland I was brought along here first. "You're going on a ni-ice trip to the Continent," they said. And inside of twelve hours I was parked at Zürich. I quite like it there,' Terence went on, 'but that ain't the point. I was decoyed.' The whole building was alive it seemed, with similar lowering memories. Esme saw the point. It was the half-way house for disaster. 'Now down at Badlock, it's peaceful. The air's so thick you can hide away behind it, and Madame Fairweather keeps her trap closed for five minutes in a day. Up here it's different. Everybody's on top of everybody and knows where everybody is. They whisper away from breakfast to dinner. They're always up to that, of course, but at Badlock you don't hear 'em.'

Once again, Esme saw the point. St Ambrose Gate was too small for Sandra, her personality filled the house, you couldn't move an inch without impinging on it. This led to everything becoming magnified and menacing.

'And your mother – ?' began Esme.

'Aw, let's have a drink and forget her,' said Terence.

It was no good, thought Esme. He was in such complete agreement with all that Terence's remark implied. Before he knew where he was there would be an atmosphere of complicity – of conspiracy, indeed, and at Sandra's expense. It wouldn't take Terence long to bring him round. They were the same breed, that was the trouble, the same robust, unscrupulous, and self-indulgent breed. They had some Coca-Cola, which turned out to be an oddly attractive drink and made Esme feel still more friendly. And then Sandra came and swept them off to the Savoy.

At the Savoy Sandra said, 'I've got to go to Canada for a week in a day or two. You two can be at Badlock. We'll drive there tomorrow afternoon, and I'll come back on Saturday.' Esme blinked. Terence remained impassive – he had heard this sort of thing before.

'When I get back,' she went on, 'we'll talk over what you're to do. Mr Sa Foy and I thought sailing would be such fun, darling.' Terence still remained impassive. If you declined to discuss a thing Sandra soon forgot it. But if you did start talking, whether you used intelligence or temper, whether you had a scene or a friendly

54

argument, the thing would stick in her mind and might even turn into a reality. Sailing was a thoroughly typical craze, he considered. But the way Esme was simpering soon reassured him. He agreed that it might be fun.

In the middle of dinner, Sandra said she was going to ring up Colonel Heffer in hospital. She'd be back before long.

'She'll make us late,' said Terence furiously, and then : 'I think sailing would be such fun, don't you?'

'No,' said Esme, 'I don't.'

'So that's all right. Anything else on the stocks?'

'Biarritz perhaps.'

'Suits me. But she'll string along as well if we go there.'

Esme made a last and despairing attempt at loyalty.

'I think she's great fun.' As a matter of fact, he did.

'Great fun my ——,' said Terence : 'if she'd only lay a few eggs, she might have something to cackle about.'

Esme giggled. Mrs Fairweather came back with a packet which she said was special melon seeds the head-waiter had given her.

'Keep them safely, darling,' she said, and handed them to Terence, who threw them under the table.

'The thing is this, dears,' she announced, 'I must go and see Ronnie about half-way through the film. But I'll get back before the end and you can both tell me what's happened.'

The bill came. Among other things, it said ten shillings for melons. Sandra flew into a rage.

'What might this be, pray?' she enquired of a passing waiter who had been serving a totally different table. He went to see. Ten minutes later the head waiter came, but Sandra was ringing up Mrs Valley to say how diabolical the Savoy was. Twenty minutes later she came back. Terence was fuming. 'We'll miss the film,' he said.

'Don't be selfish and extravagant, Terence. You can't go sweeping off and pay ten shillings for nothing at all. Mr Sa Foy, you must teach Terence money-sense. The whole thing's typical. Cinema, cinema, cinema, pay, pay, pay. Here I am enquiring why I'm being cheated, and all you do is grumble.'

It turned out that melons meant melon seeds.

'But this is ridiculous – they were a present.' And indeed they were by the time she had said her say.

They arrived when the film was half over and bought three

nine-shilling seats. 'Never be able to find you downstairs.') Sandra went straight off to see Colonel Heffer.

'Where are the melon seeds?' said Esme.

'In the Savoy Grill,' said Terence.

Sandra got back in time for God Save the King. 'But this is absurd, we've been cheated,' she said. 'I understood it was the small picture when we got here.'

'The man did say – ,' began Esme.

'Well I'm having my nine shillings back, anyway, didn't see a thing.'

The box office was shut, they said.

She supposed someone had a key.

But everyone had gone home.

No one else would till she had her nine shillings.

In the end the commissionaire (a lover of peace) gave Sandra nine shillings of his own, which she happily accepted.

'Where are those precious melon seeds?'

'You had them,' said Terence and Esme.

'Ring up the cinema, Mr Sa Foy, and ask if they've found any melon seeds.'

They hadn't.

'Try the Savoy.'

Yes, beneath madam's table they had found . . .

'How in hell did they get there? You'd better drive round at once, no time tomorrow.'

Esme took a taxi and retrieved the melon seeds.

'It's a funny thing, I thought I gave them to Terence. He said no, I put them in my lap . . . I wonder if it's one of his . . . I *know*: he was going to go back there tomorrow, say he'd come from me, that I didn't want them after all, and please to give him the money back.'

'But they were free,' said Esme.

But Sandra was too angry to notice.

'You see,' she said, 'the kind of thing I have to put up with.'

# V

The next morning, when Esme and Terence were having breakfast (Sandra never got up till about twelve) the secretary arrived. She was a youngish woman with the 'Indian Army wife' sort of look, which generally comes from having a husband in a supposedly responsible position and the certain knowledge that he will probably have to go behind a counter in Marks & Spencer on his retirement. Her first husband had indeed been doing something in the African police but his abilities had warranted employment only in the least salubrious districts, and the end of all his efforts for promotion was a fatal dose of fever.

On her return to London, Mrs Donovan as she had then been called had been duped (she was made for it) into marrying a succulent rascal called Chaser. At the time he appeared to have a good deal of money. This he may or may not have had, but he certainly had another wife. For the time being, however, all went well. The other wife did not appear while the evidences of a considerable income did. They included a wedding present to Mrs Chaser in the form of a large Bentley.

For some months she lived happily enough in a fool's paradise and a succession of night clubs. One day, however, a large cheque Chaser had written appeared on the breakfast table with a not very polite request for an explanation. This in itself was simple enough. He had run through his own money and all Mrs Chaser's savings as well – he had asked her to hand them over for investment. Why he had taken the trouble to improve her sense of security with a Bentley nobody ever found out. Perhaps he had a good heart. But even then the exchange had been a good one, for Mrs Chaser's little bit of cash had amounted to £6,000-odd, what with legacies and the Savings Bank, while the Bentley was of a

57

none too recent year and second-hand at that. But second-hand or not, it was all there was to meet the crisis – a point that Chaser, whose experience of such situations was considerable, was not slow to appreciate. By lunch-time the following day he and the Bentley had driven out of Mrs Chaser's life for ever, leaving only a lugubrious succession of bad cheques, which appeared by every post in inexorable sequence, and a note to explain that her name was still in fact Donovan, so that financial claims at any rate were out.

If Mrs Chaser was not responsible for the cheques, she was for herself. A job was the only thing. It so happened that about this time Mrs Fairweather had caught the sixteenth secretary embezzling the stamp money; and as her name was triply black-listed by every agency in London, had been compelled to advertise. Mrs Chaser appeared in answer, mercifully retaining enough of the Indian widow look to be considered sound, and got the job along with her first square meal for a week.

Now when Mrs Chaser had first been taken on, though she had been depressed by the inadequacy of Donovan and disillusioned by the villainy of his successor, she had still been a fairly normal woman. That is to say she believed in England, in overdrafts, in the Navy League and in God, which for a woman of her class and upbringing is what might have been expected. Sandra soon changed all that. It was not that the paperwork was excessive, though what with the constant flux of servants and prolonged correspondence about bills in which Sandra was being cheated, it was apt to be a bit muddled. It was the house at St Ambrose Gate which finished Mrs Chaser, and above all the one most terrifying and maddening feature of it – the incessant and prolonged telephone calls.

These started on her arrival at 9.30 every morning. From then until 5 p.m. a never-ending succession of tradesmen, lawyers, friends and relations, enemies and anonymous beggars kept the telephone in her office wailing like all the lost souls in unison. Nor had the unhappy woman been born with the knack of spotting the essential end of a conversation and making firmly and laconically towards it. She would get bogged down, like her employer, in complicated irrelevances and heart-breaking appendices without ever discussing the main point at all. This meant that either the call was repeated a few minutes later or else that she herself had to ring back. The second, she found, was almost worse. For she was developing a neurotic horror of the telephone, and to approach it in cold blood and without immediate compulsion was almost more than she could bear. The influence of the instrument was eating into her health, her brain and her soul. After a month she was an embittered woman and rapidly on the way to becoming a dangerous one.

All this may seem comparatively unimportant : but it meant that Esme, try how he might, had an enemy in the house from the start. Everything about him was calculated to antagonize the wretched Mrs Chaser, who, whereas in better days she would rather have liked him, was now conscious to the depths of her corroded being first of Esme's purely amateur status as a wage earner, secondly of the preferable nature of his employment, and thirdly and above all of the fact that his salary was considerably higher than her own – the more so as he had all found, while she lived in what had once been a tart's flat in Battersea. Then there was a further twist to the situation. Mrs Chaser and Mrs Valley had at once recognized in each other fellow-members of the downtrodden section of the gentility. They were in alliance – an alliance formed by envy, hatred, and avarice. Mrs Valley had Sandra's ear in a social way, Mrs Chaser had it by way of business. Where one fell down the other moved in. Mrs Chaser could complain about Esme's expense accounts, Mrs Valley about his behaviour. As a combination they were unassailable. And though no word passed between them on the subject, they did not need to tell each other that a new tutor was, for different reasons, fair and desirable game for both.

But all this had yet to be made plain to Esme, who put on his very best act of 'I'm just a little boy, please won't you mother me?' and minced round her office between telephone calls asking what he could do. Terence and he were finally packed off for the morning with a minute cheque to be cashed (which was one way of getting them out of the house) and otherwise complete *carte blanche*.

The consequence of this was that they had soon arrived at Merlin's Bookstore, St Martin's Lane, where Terence intended to refurnish his stock of pulp literature.

It had, Esme found, its compensations. While Terence was ferreting away amidst a selection of space-ships, corpses, and women with anti gamma-ray discs on their breasts, he himself was

59

at leisure to explore a considerable range of pornography, permanent and ephemeral. The permanent stuff was the usual stock-in-trade of sixth-formers everywhere, but the periodicals were of more interest. To start with, they were all sealed to the public gaze by a piece of sticky tape (all, that is, except for provoking covers of people on swings who were wearing silk stockings). Secondly, he noticed that they ranged back in date to considerably before the war, and that whereas yesterday's productions were going for five shillings, last year's would be up to ten, and those of the last decade could seldom be bought for under two pounds. Here, too, it seemed at first, there was a collector's snobbery of age.

But this was only in part the explanation. What happened, it appeared, was that you made your purchase and carried it bashfully away, but if you brought it back again you received half-price. It was then sealed up to await another client. The result was that you could develop a permanent, if intermittent, affection for a certain issue, which could be resold and rebought indefinitely. As time went on, of course, the man explained to Esme, certain issues tended to disappear or else to become so thoroughly thumbed that they really had to go out of circulation. Accordingly someone who was deeply devoted to the 1938 number of *Paris ce Soir* might find there were only about two copies still in existence, and was therefore prepared, since affection of this nature for some reason died very hard, to pay a stiff price for a week with his old favourite. From his long acquaintance he was prepared to give a personal recommendation of the bosoms of '39 vintage and the bottoms of '35. Should Esme be interested, he could even – Esme hurriedly bought something of very recent date for the good of the house, and went to find Terence.

Terence had supplied himself with a pile of magazines about a foot and a half high, and a few American dailies of the previous week.

'Whatever do you want these for?' said Esme.

'Might come in handy,' was the vague answer. 'Documents of historical interest perhaps.'

'But whatever'd your mother say, spending all this money on back dailies. Comics are one thing, but these . . . And who's to pay?'

'You,' said Terence : 'the expense account can bear the charge of a taxi here and some tea there which will soon cover this lot –

and that,' he added, eyeing poor Esme's copy of *Tit for Tat* with a look of unfeigned complicity.

'I suppose it could,' said Esme weakly; 'all I ask is that you keep it all hidden away.'

'I put them under her bed,' said Terence : 'she conducts little searches of my room but as she doesn't suspect herself of buying these things she never looks in her own. Simple.'

'But supposing – ' Terence took the point.

'She's got a bathroom just next door,' he said, 'and a bladder like an ox.'

As Esme had stipulated, he was going out to lunch that day with a friend. They were then driving down to Badlock at half past three.

It was when he came out of his club after lunch, slightly unsteady and having left his friend to sleep it off, that a most peculiar thing happened. Drawn up at the bottom of the steps was a large black Rolls with an immaculate chauffeur standing by it. The man whipped his cap off and placed it under his arm.

'Mr Esme Sa Foy?' he said. Esme nodded.

'Get in, if you please, sir. We are rather late.'

God, thought Esme to himself, Mrs Fairweather in a last-minute hurry, and here he was keeping her waiting and rather tight. Had he been less so, he would have recalled that Mrs Fairweather had no black Rolls, for the time being no chauffeur, and no knowledge of where he was lunching. After about five minutes of going in what even he saw to be the wrong direction, something of this nature did indeed occur to him.

'Where are we going?' he asked.

'I do assure you, sir,' said the chauffeur, 'that everything is all right. You'll be back in good time to leave for the country.'

One might as well, supposed Esme, spend the interim riding in someone else's Rolls as standing about tight at 6, St Ambrose Gate.

'Very well,' he said.

Meanwhile they had crossed Oxford Street and were weaving about in a network of roads alternately opulent and shabby. Finally they drew up in front of a block of flats in Hallam Street.

'Here we are, sir,' said the chauffeur.

Esme followed him into a lift which seemed to do everything

automatically except play music. They left it at the sixth floor, and proceeded silently down a series of passages as complicated as Minos' labyrinth. When they eventually stopped in front of an unnumbered door, the chauffeur pressed the bell and vanished – almost as magically as the Slave of the Lamp and without a smell of cordite. The door was opened by a gross man in an unpleasant suit.

'Mr Sa Foy?' said a fruity voice.

'Yes.'

'Come in please.'

Esme followed him into a luxuriously – and tastefully – appointed sitting-room. The fixtures were cleverly chosen and the sideboard was loaded with all the many-coloured bottles that puzzle and delight travellers in a French bar.

'Sit down please, Mr Sa Foy. You will require, I suppose, both apologies and explanations. And an introduction,' he added thoughtfully : 'You shall have them all, dear boy, you shall have them all. I am Mr Chynnon, Mr Edward Chynnon; this is not my normal place of residence, you understand, just a little – er – something I keep in the background. Apologies therefore for bringing you here – and so suddenly, dear boy.'

Something clicked in Esme's memory.

' "Eddie" Chynnon?' he enquired.

'To some, Mr Sa Foy,' said Mr Chynnon, raising his eyebrows; 'I see you have heard of me. From your employer?'

Esme thought so.

'Quite, I understand she is rather fond of bringing me into the conversation?' he tilted a blotchy scalp towards Esme.

Esme wouldn't know. It had only happened once, and in any case he hardly knew Mrs Fairweather.

'That is exactly the point, Mr Sa Foy. Time is short, and I am grateful to you for raising it so quickly. You hardly know her and yet you have heard her discuss me. Now tell me, dear boy, was the context of a disparaging nature?'

'It was a bit,' admitted Esme.

'That is again the point. Now I must tell you, dear boy, that I have reason to believe, in fact I know, that your employer is in the habit of constantly making such statements at my expense. Constantly and publicly. Such things can do one a good deal of harm – especially,' he said more fruitily than ever, 'if there is some grain – you are a man of the world, Mr Sa Foy – some small grain of truth in what is said, sufficient, shall we say, to prevent one taking any sort of action that might make public what is liable to misinterpretation.'

Here he allowed himself a repulsive look of self-connivance.

'Now tell me, Mr Sa Foy, as a young man who has had his ups and downs (I have made wide enquiries, you need deny nothing), how would you yourself react to such a situation? What steps would it occur to you to take?'

'I don't really know,' said Esme : 'for one thing, what reason has she for this? If you could discover that, make amends, and then ask her to put it about that she had been mistaken . . .'

'Passable in theory, dear boy – that I admit. But in the first place I fancy her motive for such talk, if it is not the mere wantonness of an idle mind, is so deeply entangled in a neurotic and restless nature – a fancied slight perhaps – that nothing will serve to root it out, let alone convince her that it was baseless.

'And in any case,' he went on, 'even supposing she should agree to make it publicly known she had been misled, no one, after months of such pleasurable gossip, would go to the pains of believing her renunciation. Dirt sticks, dear boy – as who should know better than you? No, the damage is done : remember that, dear boy, whatever happens the damage is done. Think again, if you please.'

'There's only one thing left for me to think,' said Esme, ' – that whatever steps you took would be for personal satisfaction rather than actual redress of wrong.'

'Precisely, dear boy – I have in fact no alternative but to equate the two. And what do you deduce from this?'

'I suppose that there is very little you can do except repay her in her own currency.'

'But such intelligence,' cried Mr Chynnon. 'I must ask you, however, to soften your term a little. No more of Repayment, dear boy, I beg of you – such primitive and biblical associations. Justice, there is the keyword – one must become the agent of justice. And indeed what more could one ask? An interest independent of the years, a positively objective occupation – not to say intellectual, for in what terms does justice deal save those of the truth? Yes,' he said, 'the truth, Mr Sa Foy. You take my meaning?'

'Not entirely,' said Esme.

'Well then, dear boy, I must explain to you. "Repayment in her own currency" was your phrase – harsh, if I may say so, coarse, without subtlety, but let it pass – very well, but what is her currency? To put it briefly, scandal. But the agent of justice cannot afford to traffick in mere scandal. Your employer has been frequently married, dear boy, but she has always been released on her own terms, she is the friend of Great Ones, her war record is an official and impressive document, she has a name for good works – in short, she is above suspicion. No mere fictions, however entertaining, will serve our – my purpose. Justice is an exact science, dear boy, and an individual act of justice, in order to be feasible, must be flawless. In other words, it must be based on Truth. Do you understand me now?'

'Perhaps,' said Esme; 'correct me if I am wrong, but it seems that in order to return Mrs Fairweather the treatment she has meted out to you, you wish to know something about her – something incontrovertible and discreditable – that may be put gently into circulation among persons of her acquaintance.' Pompousness, it seemed, was infectious.

'Right,' said Mr Chynnon, almost with a scream, 'dear boy, you are dead right.'

'Well then,' said Esme, who was roughly speaking in possession of himself, 'it is now your turn to explain. You have so far treated me to the history of a rather sordid set of circumstances, and bullied me into a deduction which, given a certain rather depraved turn of mind, was more or less tautological. Unless it is your custom to conduct elementary exercises in logic with perfect strangers, at 2.30 in the afternoon, in a flat which more nearly resembles a brothel, I imagine there is something more to come.'

'Such intelligence,' said Mr Chynnon with a cross between a sneer and a simper, 'dear boy, you are, once again, dead right.'

'Then give,' said Esme in unconscious reminiscence of Terence.

'Very well, dear boy, I will give. Please to let me have your very best attention. I must now admit that, on hearing of your recent appointment, I examined your past career both with interest and admiration. Above all you seemed to possess two qualities which the world too often allows to proceed in conjunction – intelligence and penury. This being the case, it occurred to me that you might be prepared to bear service, for a suitable reward of course, in the cause of Justice. May I add that your previous record gave me no very substantial reason to anticipate a refusal?'

'If you would care to be more concrete . . .' murmured Esme.

'But certainly. I should even care to make an offer. Mr Sa Foy,' said Edward Chynnon, 'I am prepared to offer you five pounds a week if you will do no more than assure me that during the time you are in Mrs Fairweather's service you will do your best to follow the clue I shall now give you – or any others that might come to your notice. I am aware,' he continued, 'that this may seem a small sum for difficult service in the cause of Justice. But the temples of the goddess are well stocked. Should you follow the clue I mention to a successful and final conclusion, provided of course that your result is verifiable by myself, I am prepared to – I *will* give you,' he drew a deep breath, 'the sum of one thousand pounds. No less. For a few words that will pass between us, I will give you one thousand pounds. I need hardly add that your anonymity will receive all the respect so obviously necessary in a case of this kind. What do you say to that, Mr Sa Foy?'

There was a momentary pause. Then :

'Twenty pounds in advance, no telephone calls, and all payments in cash,' said Esme, who seemed to himself to be operating on someone else's reflexes.

'Very reasonable,' said Mr Chynnon without a stir, 'very reasonable, dear boy. And in return I must stipulate that you send a fortnightly report – one must protect one's interests – a fortnightly report, no matter how brief, to an address I shall give you shortly. But all this is an irrelevance. Time is short. I must insist that you pay the strictest attention to what I am now about to tell you.

'*In primis*, then, here is an envelope containing twenty pounds, and an address which will always find me. Don't be surprised at such preparation, dear boy – you would hardly have asked for less and I would never have given more. One month from this date, provided your reports are regular and to my satisfaction, you will start receiving registered envelopes, at the rate of one a week, each containing five pound notes – and perhaps a little extra if your efforts have warranted it. So much for administration.

'However, what really concerns us at the moment is the clue I promised you. Now you will bear in mind that your task is to find some one fact that may serve as a suitable rod for the just chastisement of Mrs Fairweather. Her life has been erratic but not lubricious. Above all, her present existence, while more erratic than ever, is completely blameless. You will therefore confine your attentions to her past – and largely to one particular section of that past. Even there, I'm afraid, possibilities are few. But possibilities there are, and these I will now outline.

'Know then that your employer has had three husbands. Of these neither the first nor the last need detain us, for whatever the rights and wrongs may have been, both were divorced by her – with plenty of ill will, I don't doubt, but without resistance on their part or noticeable breach of conduct on hers. The man who concerns us is the second husband – a Mr Earl Marshal Acre, an American of wealth, reputation, chivalrous instincts, and bad blood. You may or may not know that after the honeymoon had lasted a bare three weeks he was found stone dead in the Californian hotel where they were staying. He left a note confessing to suicide – a mere confession, nothing more – and about two million dollars, which went, of course, to his wife.' He paused to take breath and prepare for an analysis. Esme did not feel up to making comment.

'Now in view of the note there is little enough possibility of foul play in anybody's case, and none at all in Mrs Fairweather's. She was already a very rich woman quite apart from anything else. What has puzzled many people since, however, is Marshal Acre's motive. He was nondescript but likeable : he had no enemies and a lot of money; and there was no suggestion of blackmail, scandal or drugs. What is more, he adored his wife, and though he was doubtless in for a fair dose of disillusion, it could hardly have come – *at any rate through the normal channels* – within three weeks. Even Sandra couldn't madden a man to the extent of suicide within that time. What then is the explanation?'

He looked wistfully at Esme.

'There has been no explanation. In fact nothing else whatever is known about it. They had friends in America, of course, but many of them disappeared in the war, and in any case I have not been able to trace one of them who was in California at the time. Nor did anyone find out anything subsequently. It was hardly the topic people introduced the moment they met her, she was entirely natural and reticent about her grief, and for that matter

66

very little was seen of her for some while afterwards. In fact most people would say I was a fool to bother about what is, on the face of it, a complete and seemingly rather dull, mystery.'

Here he leant forward as if about to say something rather remarkable. As it happened it was merely intense.

'Nevertheless, dear boy,' he said, 'I have a *hunch* about this. I have an idea that if there's any dirt going it can be traced back to that Californian honeymoon hotel. It is to this incident that I wish to direct your attention, though I must admit, dear boy, that where I promised you a clue I probably appear to be saddling for your use one big and cumbrous white elephant. Which is why the final price I offer is so high,' he added.

'But haven't you any more details,' enquired Esme from his dream, 'names, dates, places . . . ?'

Mr Chynnon shrugged his shoulders.

'I have here,' he said, 'for your use a list of the Acres' American friends, and on which you'll also find the people resident in their hotel – The Ten Ways, Palm Beach – at the time. Of the former category, the majority, as I told you, are dead, while in any case none were present at Palm Beach when the so-called tragedy occurred. As for the other guests at the hotel, they were all thoroughly investigated at the time and were in any event complete strangers to the Acres. Marshal Acre never had a girlfriend or an enemy in his life. It's dirt I want,' he said suddenly and viciously, 'not suspects.'

Realizing he had let himself down he went on more calmly : 'They none of them knew anything. The Acres had a large suite and went there, as you may have gathered, in an off season and to avoid people – even ones they knew. They weren't likely to start picking up unfashionable riff-raff. It wasn't a smart hotel, you know. As for the dates, they're all down there – they're common knowledge in any case. No,' he said, 'everything that can be done from the outside has been done. You're on the inside. A word here, a letter there' – Esme shuddered – 'who knows? Who knows, dear boy? You have a lucky face, a charming face if I may say so . . .'

He was silent for about half a minute, and then began again quickly and rather savagely –

'And it's high time you took your charming face back to Mrs Fairweather – who always misses a novelty if it's away for long.

67

My chauffeur will drop you anywhere handy – provided it's well clear of her house.'

The very sight of Esme seemed now to be filling him with nervous irritation. Esme shook hands hurriedly and was shown to the door, where the immaculate chauffeur appeared from nowhere and took him down to the car.

# VI

When Esme got to bed that night in a large and handsome bedroom at Badlock House, he had time to think things over.

Even now he had hardly recovered from the first and most obvious reaction – which was surprise. And after all he had grounds for it. He had been abducted in broad daylight and in the best Dornford Yates fashion, and had had a proposition put to him that was tantamount to criminal. Again, all this elaborate conspiracy and the vast reward it involved seemed to be focussed round the most commonplace and trivial occurrence – the use, by an excitable woman, of a few malicious but probably thoughtless words. Esme, of course, had yet to gain much insight into the methods and modes of thought of the very rich. Had he been a previous witness of the bizarre combinations of extravagance and meanness, or the endless and white-hot controversies about nothing at all, which form so large and prominent a part of their world, he would not have thought Mr Chynnon's offer so odd. For Mr Chynnon too was really very rich indeed, while the grievance he harboured was exactly the sort that is calculated to shake the houses of the first four hundred for months on end.

And indeed Sandra had rather let her tongue loose on his account. For though she had many friends of long standing among men of his type, periodically the memory of her brother's disaster would rise before her to cause a sudden and violent reaction. She would then refuse to see her equivocal friends for weeks at a time, and allow herself to develop a gnawing hatred for one or more of them and for no apparent reason at all. Before her latest little upset she had often entertained and been entertained by Edward Chynnon : but as he was really more than usually repellent, and as the target he offered was, without doubt, more than usually vulnerable, she had suddenly surprised the town with a series of references, anecdotes and innuendoes which, by the sheer naked quality of their malice, excelled anything in their kind that the last twenty years could show. The result was that Sandra's remarks had received the well-deserved compliment of being incessantly repeated over a period of months and in every nook, corner and cloakroom of the first ten hotels in London. It was not surprising that some of them had come round to Mr Chynnon, and still less surprising that he appeared a trifle restless under their lash. Nor could he be blamed altogether if the accumulations of such lashes began, after a week or two, to turn his restlessness into anger and then his anger into fury. Esme, of course, could hardly grasp the full force of the situation at so early a stage of his acquaintance with it; but a more detailed knowledge of the circumstances would have explained most things and a deeper insight into the constitution of Mr Chynnon and his immediate circle would have accounted for all.

But if he had yet to realize the full extent of the devastating waves of hysteria that sweep in continuous succession across the world he was now entering, he had already received a sort of opiate inoculation from Sandra that was beginning to atrophy his faculty for amazement. Nor, for the matter of that, had he any illusions about the potential vileness of mankind. His surprise therefore was not as strong as it might have been, and was speedily giving place to another emotion – that of resentment. For when he thought over what had happened, he decided that his assent to Mr Chynnon's little scheme had been entirely taken for granted – and by himself as much as by Mr Chynnon. Like all people of easy virtue, he resented being taken for granted – he liked to preserve the illusion that he had certain standards if he cared to use them. He was particularly annoyed with himself : for whether it was the lunch, the surprise, or the impact of Mr Chynnon's personality, he had given his immediate consent without thought, word, or gesture. 'What do you say to that, Mr Sa Foy?' – and he had grabbed at it with both hands. One should try to put a price on oneself – that was his rule; and for all practical purposes it was on the way to becoming as otiose as the laws of Solon.

On this point, however, he managed by degrees to reassure himself. For if he had refused, Mr Chynnon, who seemed to know his record, would probably have threatened to submit that record to Mrs Fairweather. It was a specious argument, but it raised yet a further question – the first of a long list of half-digested doubts. Where the devil did Mr Chynnon get all his information? It was a simple matter to trace someone's past history: but how did he know about Esme's appointment as tutor? Above all, how did he come to be so well apprised as to his almost hourly movements? Had he another member of Mrs Fairweather's house in his payment? But Esme had told no one, not even Terence, where he was having lunch. Very well then, had he private detectives in his employment? And if so, how did they discover that Mrs Fairweather, Terence, and Esme were driving down to Badlock that day? On second thoughts, however, this was an easy one. A casual word with one of the servants would soon have revealed that. But it occurred to Esme that they must be private detectives of a peculiarly shady sort, at any rate if they were acquainted with Mr Chynnon's motives.

And here was another point. What were his motives? Himself had explained them as the discovery of something discreditable about Sandra to be circulated among her friends. It might just as well be blackmail. If so, he, Esme, would be an accomplice; and while he had no rooted objection to blackmail as such, he had no particular wish to end up in prison.

This again raised the whole question of his safety. A bird in hand, after all, he said to himself, and just let Mrs Fairweather catch him meddling about with letters and things for a prize disaster. On the other hand, if Mr Chynnon was so well informed, it was on the cards he would go on being so. What would happen if Esme did nothing at all? Mr Chynnon's payment would stop, doubtless, but even worse might happen. He might, for example, take delayed action by way of revealing Esme's really remarkable unfittedness for his employment. He might start blackmailing Esme. He might even have Esme's throat cut, thought Esme, as Badlock was doubtless full of people who would cut their mothers' throats for the asking. No, this was getting morbid, out of proportion – no one would get his throat cut, pull yourself together. The fact remained, however, that the situation, so gleefully accepted along with twenty pounds in an envelope, was more complex than comfortable. One must decide on a line of action as consistent as possible with peace of mind and stick to it come what might.

71

After two days' thought it seemed to Esme (who had so far seen no one who even remotely resembled an agent of Mr Chynnon's) that comfort and profit might be sought in concert. Whatever happened he had the twenty pounds (it had been rather like snatching money in a dream and waking up to find it in your hand), and this would be a great help to him in fulfilling the Bursar's demands. The thousand-pound jackpot was remote to say the least of it and might most properly be left to the disposal of the devil, whose instrument it doubtless was. But without in any way compromising himself with Mrs Fairweather, he could easily dispatch a series of non-committal, intelligent, and even apparently hopeful reports that should serve to bring in a little extra money later. It was rather a spiritless decision, he supposed, but really he was entirely alien soil, having never been either a tutor or a private agent before. He would send in his reports and otherwise leave things to take their course. And with this rather stagnant resolution, he settled down to inconvenience himself as little as possible for the ensuing nine weeks.

But the stars in their courses had no intention whatever of providing Esme with an easy summer.

In the first place, there was the marked difficulty of living life in the same house as Mrs Fairweather. She had an uncanny faculty for knowing what went on – even at Badlock, where the house and garden between them should have given sufficient concealment for a century of undiscovered crime. The richer people are the more they want their money's worth, and the mere suspicion that Terence and Esme might be up to no good was enough to set the internal telephone ringing along every corridor. During the day Esme could never sit on his bottom with anything like a sense of security, and to lose sight of Terence amounted to high treason. Then there would be the most exhausting rows about anything from the loss of a nice table-mat to the discovery of an unsuspected horsewhip – which, it was presumed, had been imported by Terence to repeat the outrage on the gardener's boy. Such trifles were only settled by a complete disruption of all domestic system and economy. Until the mat was found, there would be no meals – the entire staff were looking for the mat. Until it was discovered that the horsewhip (a long-forgotten present) in fact bore Mrs Fairweather's initials, there would be no peace for anyone till the entire house had been searched (secretly of course, for Terence must not know of it) for more concealed horsewhips. Many things of interest came to light this way, and a good half of them provided material for further rows, searches, telephone calls and conferences. Esme found that, like an officer of the Brigade of Guards he must never show signs of fatigue. It was all a bit rough on the nerves.

Secondly, there was the difficulty of life with Terence. The difficulty here was of a different sort. It is of course always rather lowering to be with the same person every hour of every day, but as Terence was, for his age, an intelligent and very amusing child, this was not the immediate trouble. The trouble was to prevent him baiting his mother and thus discrediting his tutor. Now Terence had taken a liking to the indulgent Esme (he was on, he foresaw, to a very profitable thing), and was anxious therefore to treat him fairly gently, trick him into a position of complete complicity and not give cause for complaint against him. But even with this in mind, his mother was a target irresistible to the saints themselves. The very sight of her as she flew off after imaginary horsewhips or rampaged around in search of disappearing table-mats tickled his sense of humour so much that he could hardly stand. It was too much to expect of human nature that he should refrain from providing a few artificial situations of his own ingenious manufacture to recreate the same effects. It was also too much to expect of human nature that when Sandra returned from a prolonged conference with the local doctor to find Terence prostrate on the floor with a packet of tablets that have the well-known effect of turning the intestinal acids a bright scarlet, she should take it lying down. Even the excuse that he had only intended to try them on her favourite dachshund did no good. Esme was summoned for a raging scene, the vividness of which was only increased by the simplicity and antiquity of the way she had been duped. No, it was not at all easy on the nerves.

However, on the Saturday after their arrival at Badlock, it really looked as though peace was to be restored. At twelve o'clock Esme, who was just beginning to wonder how much money a suitable rest-cure in September would necessitate, was summoned to Sandra's bedroom and told that she was off to spend the week-end with the Marquess of Luton Hoo, proposed proceeding thence to London, and from London to Montreal. She would be in Canada a week. Esme must manage servants, house, drink, cars and cash till her return – and must drive Terence to London on Monday, where Dr McTavish wished to see what difference another term in Switzerland had made, and where they could wish God's speed to herself before she flew away. She also remembered to warn him that Bellamy was coming on long leave from Eton the following week-end, and that in all probability he could expect another week-end visitor in the person of Dr Trito, who, at a cost of a round fifty pounds, also wished to assess the recent progress of Terence. Would he please call her Sandra (S,A,N,D,R,A), because his everlasting 'Mrs Fairweathers' were making her feel about ninety? She had decided she both liked him and placed confidence in him she might add. They would forget the incident of the unfortunate pills.

Having delivered herself of this condensed series of instructions, she got into the powder-blue Rolls and drove away. At noon she was there and at twelve-fifteen she wasn't. Terence and Esme heaved a sigh; and went in to celebrate with a couple of double gins. The rest-cure, it seemed, could be enjoyed in instalments and while Esme was still being employed. With the exception of Monday, ten days of perfect peace were before him.

But ironically enough it was that afternoon on which a third factor in the situation made its appearance, and finally shattered every idea of repose Esme had been rash enough to retain.

It all fell out very simply. After lunch it rained with all the persistence and gloom peculiar to the fenlands, so that Terence and Esme (who had in any case intended to do nothing at all) went gratefully into the lounge to spend their first afternoon of stationary peace for some days. Esme, in particular, welcomed the chance of absorbing some of his necessary drug, print, which he had so far been consistently denied.

What with the time of day and the weather something fairly light was called for; and he accordingly went up to his bedroom, where there were displayed two rows of fiction suitable to week-end visitors, and pounced on a copy of *Caprice*. It had been left there, it seemed, sometime ago: for on the inside of the cover appeared the name William Gomery, followed by a date, 1936. Esme blessed Mr William Gomery and his forgetful nature with all his heart, and went to join Terence, who was busy tormenting the dachshund with a knitting-needle and drawing a picture of four masked men disembowelling a cow with their fingernails.

At page fifty Esme was provided with a thrill that had nothing to do with Firbank. He turned the page to find a letter – a short note on only one side of a small piece of handsome paper. At the top was written '3.30 a.m., Sunday morning'. Now it was a custom of Sandra's to retire to her room about midnight and then to stay awake till four o'clock or later reading and writing letters. One morning Esme had found four different sets of contradictory instructions on the breakfast table, dated respectively 12.30, 1.15, 2.45, and 3. This habit was evidently of long standing, for the note now before him was also in Sandra's hand, though he noticed that it had been firmer in those days, and that the dashes she used to introduce an inconsequence were less frequent. It began without heading – a common trick of Sandra's even in full-dress letters.

'You can't imagine,' it said, 'the relief it has been to me to find someone, after all this time, in whom my intuition permits me to confide. Few people seem to have sympathy – of your own sex next to none. So I feel I must send you this to thank you, my dear Bill, and tell you how happy you have made me. The fact you can say what you have means all the more to me when I remember how fond you were of poor Earl.

Your everlasting grateful friend,<br>Sandra.'

As Esme was on the verge of going to sleep, for a moment or so his reactions were merely the mechanical ones of construing four sentences. Sandra had been seeking advice or consolation and had been afforded a diplomatic reception. He closed his eyes, the word 'Earl' went through his brain like a needle, he slammed the book and bolted for his own room. There he read the note again, slowly and carefully.

So there was something, it appeared, in Mr Chynnon's hunch. Or there might be. Examine the evidence. *In primis*, there was something worth confiding ('in whom my intuition permits me to confide') – but was there? Sandra would write twenty notes if she confided a mole on her bottom. Well, whatever it was, it concerned the late Mr Marshal Acre ('how fond you were of poor Earl') of chivalrous instincts and bad blood. (Perhaps he had a mole on his bottom.) Gomery had said something which she valued, the more because he was a friend of Acre's. But then he could be valued as such without her confidences necessarily concerning Acre. Unlikely. The interview had taken place during or since 1936 – when Gomery had treated himself to a copy of *Caprice*. Sentimental memories would be failing; one could say, 'I like what you said because you knew Acre,' only if what had been said was *about* Acre – especially if one had only been married to Acre three weeks. Finally there was someone else who knew (if he was still living) what it was all about. Mr William Gomery, who read Firbank – who was also a friend of Sandra's. Find Gomery. Win a thousand pounds. Let Chynnon find Gomery – and send someone else to win a thousand pounds. Forget the thousand pounds and expect a handsome bonus for being smart. 'Dear Mr Chynnon, after a laborious and dangerous search in Mrs Fairweather's private escritoire (to break it open I had to buy a jemmy, price twenty-two shillings and sixpence) I discovered that . . .'

*Nitwit:* wait a day or two, and try to find out where Gomery lives – he might live in Badlock – or Tahiti. But worth a few days' wait and see. ONE THOUSAND POUNDS.

If Esme succeeded in saving sixty pounds, he would be well on his way to paying his college account. The unfortunate thing was that he had a level three hundred pounds worth of additional debts. Some of these, of course, were private and could wait – but one liked to do the right thing by one's friends. Others again were owed to tradesmen. Now Esme had long since discovered that compliments and charm will be accepted in lieu of the most substantial payments – indeed he had discovered it so long ago that he had allowed his method to grow stale. There were tradesmen pressing – acknowledging compliments of course, but still pressing. This meant shortage of wines, books, food, clothes and even, on occasion, sleep. It was quite intolerable.

Despite all this, Esme had felt little excitement when Chynnon had first named his figure. There was no doubt in Esme's mind that the old wretch would pay, but he might just as well have made an offer for the Holy Grail. The Acre business was incredibly remote both in space and time, everyone seemed to be dead, even the hotel, according to Esme's meagre sheet of information, had been burnt down. The Holy Grail did at least have a place in literature.

But the Gomery note was a positive searchlight in this black abyss of ignorance. If Gomery was still alive, there was a way – steep, no doubt, but a way. Gomery was a friend of Sandra's . . . Gomery *knew*. Here was his text. From now on Esme had an absorbing interest in his job, his surroundings, his employer, in everything. He was playing for a handsome stake; and was prepared to wager a good deal – including his peace of mind.

He was confirmed in his resolution by something that happened the next day. He must try his hand, he had decided, at eliciting information without arousing suspicion. For this purpose Terence had the dual advantage of being uncommonly sharp and yet of comparative unimportance in the tissue that was being woven. It would be a stimulating and completely safe test.

Terence had been dragged to church (in accordance with a frantic 'phone call from his mother, who had been 'thinking about Religion' on her way to stay with the Marquess) and had come home very voluble on the subject of the licence apparently given in these matters to boys of his age in America.

This went on till well into tea. Then Esme, who saw that anything remotely in the nature of a suspicion would be firmly held down by the prior claims of greed, made his first attack.

'Do you know many Americans?' he asked.

'Some at school,' said Terence, 'great guys.'

'I suppose so. Surely your mother must have a lot of American friends – she's lived there a lot?'

'Yeah, she's got several.' He put an entire cake into his mouth.

'Do you meet many of them?'

'Yeah. There's Uncle Bill for a start.'

'Who's Uncle Bill?'

'Uncle Bill Gomery. Old friend of mother's. Used to come here a lot – he's Bellamy's godfather, not an uncle really, just called that.'

He scooped at the chocolate biscuits.

'But is he American?' said Esme.

Terence began choking. He went red in the face and tears came to his eyes. Esme forbore to comment on the just reward of greed.

'Sure,' said Terence rather thickly when the fit had passed. 'Comes to Europe most summers though. Bellamy and I used to

77

reckon he carried a torch for mother, but it didn't lead anywhere.'

'It' may not have, but the conversation did. For the first thing Esme had done when he found out that Gomery had known Acre was to check him on Mr Chynnon's list of American friends of the newly-weds. The list was lengthy, despite the excisions of death, but Gomery's name was absent. Esme had then assumed that Gomery must be English – after all Firbank was not an American taste and Earl Marshal Acre had travelled a good deal. But this evening's conversation, which had only been intended in origin as a means to a general picture of the set-up, had now revealed unquestionably that Mr Chynnon, the very knowledge-able Mr Chynnon and all his private detectives had slipped – and very badly at that. They had missed a personal friend of Acre's, who had more recently given signs of 'carrying the torch' for Sandra.

This was both significant and encouraging. Above all, encourag-ing, because it meant that Esme could pursue his researches in full confidence of being the only person in the running. The course was admittedly no less arduous than before, but it was something to be involved in an endurance test and not in a race, and it was everything to know that there was a tangible if distant goal. The more Esme thought of it, the more incredible his fortune seemed. A fluke of the first order in his favour and an oversight of the most colossal magnitude on the part of Mr Chynnon. Jemmies for twenty-two and sixpence, indeed! Perilous antics in the escritoire! Gratuities for being smart! Mr Chynnon should have his report – a nice, orderly, polite, intelligent report, from which he would learn only what was good for him. Esme was on the trail – alone. What was more he meant to remain so. Let Mr Chynnon see to the paying out, and confine himself to that.

# VII

The next day being Monday they drove off to London as instructed.

There they found scenes of unspeakable confusion which went by the name of 'Mrs Fairweather's preparations'. Inasmuch as her visit to Canada had been announced for a week one might have thought that these would be of a simple nature. As it was they involved everything from mislaid tickets to a mislaid lady's maid (who was apparently coming too), and also included both the Valleys, who flitted about with looks of importance and were allowed to issue instructions about minor articles of luggage. Somebody from Wimpole Street was upstairs prescribing tablets against every conceivable emergency: while as for the wretched Mrs Chaser, had she had a hundred heads they would all have been needed for different telephones. She would be engaged in taking a particularly urgent in-call, when there would suddenly be a paroxysm of screams from the bedroom which were meant to convey to her a name, number and message to be immediately transmitted out. As the telephone rang again the moment it was put down, the out-messages were getting a bit behind hand. Since most of these concerned the location of the tickets, this was perhaps a pity.

Hanging about on the edge of the Snake Pit, sulky and ignored, was Dr McTavish. The moment he saw Terence he congratulated him fatuously on his growth since their last meeting, and led him away for cross-examination. Esme hid in the lavatory.

Quarter of an hour later a great scream of 'Mr Sa Foy' was heard from Sandra, and they went together to join McTavish in conference.

'I'm afraid,' said Dr McTavish, 'that I have rather grave news for you, Mrs Fairweather, but if you've no objection, I should like Mr Sa Foy to hear it.'

Sandra, who was thinking about the lady's maid, said she couldn't care less about Mr Sa Foy hearing it.

'Well then,' said the doctor in a huff – he had been waiting all morning to assert *his* importance, and it was now obvious that he could pronounce Terence permanently insane for all anybody cared – 'well then,' he said, 'his illness, while it has taken a new turn, is more deeply rooted than ever in a love of violence. In fact this new turn *in itself* indicates that he is seeking, with the dawn of an adult intelligence, to put his love of violence into a compact and rational form full of colour and appeal.' He paused dramatically. 'The new turn his illness has taken, the new vessel, as it were, from which he may draw substance for endless and corrosive fantasies, is nothing more nor less than an all-embracing *Americanism*. Clothes, films, habits, accent – all are to be chosen on the grounds of the overwhelming superiority, as he conceives it, of everything American.'

He need not have worried. Here he had Mrs Fairweather well and truly on the hop. She was not unduly disturbed by talk of 'corrosive fantasies' or 'vessels for violence', but one thing she had always determined – Terence and Bellamy were to be brought up as good, sound English boys, a credit to their mother and the Royal Family. The fact that she herself had spent years in America, the fact that she had had an American husband, the fact that she had dumped the boys in America during the entire war – all this was nothing. Since the final blasting of her matrimonial career and her voracious recapture of Terence and Bellamy, since, in short, she had begun to pay them something like consistent attention, one thing had been for certain – they were hers, and she was English, and therefore they were and would remain utterly and uncompromisingly English. A simple syllogism : it worked for Bellamy, therefore it could and must work for Terence. Dr McTavish had managed to make himself felt at last.

'How long will it last?' she enquired grimly. McTavish stroked his hair – a nugatory gesture.

'I'm afraid it's impossible to say,' he said. 'It all depends on influence, environment, above all on treatment. I think I can say that the condition will probably not be permanent. Beyond that . . .'

'Then what do you suggest?' she asked.

McTavish put the ends of his fingers together.

'I have been giving the matter some thought,' he began, 'and I think what is required is a more rigid adherence to the principles I suggested last time I was speaking to yourself and Mr Sa Foy. It is essential, in my view, that he be saturated in what we may call Englishness – that is to say English places, English people, English culture, above all English pastimes,' said the pompous and transparent buffoon : 'this means that we must now doubly emphasize the importance of athletic activity and well-ordered hours. Routine and occupation, that is the thing; where possible, of course, occupation with a definite appeal. If you remember, I suggested sailing. This, of course, is an international pastime, but it has an essentially English flavour – especially if it is undertaken in the right surroundings. It is a sport that should appeal to any boy, it requires concentration and effort. In the circumstances it should be ideal. Now what arrangements, Mrs Fairweather, have you decided on for the summer?'

'I'd thought about Biarritz,' said Sandra.

McTavish winced a little and pressed his fingers together more firmly than ever.

'In many ways an admirable idea,' he said : 'a change of scene, bathing, a different culture to be examined. But at the moment I should say Biarritz might well prove a deleterious influence. It is full of restless and unbalanced people who do not appreciate the value of routine, there is an atmosphere of prevailing levity in moral questions – and there is a prominent American section. Should Terence go there he must necessarily see condoned or even encouraged much that you would wish him to avoid. I should like to suggest that you think over the possibility of changing your plans, of sending him to an entirely English environment – such as,' he concluded without batting an eyelid, 'Aldeburgh.'

'I shall think about it in my 'plane,' said Sandra. The call of Biarritz was obviously strong, and it was far from evident that she was prepared to allow Terence's moral health a priority. Still, the new revelation about Americanism, which she had imagined to be merely a surface craze, was obviously leaving its mark.

'Yes,' she said, 'I shall think it all over very carefully.'

She then went shrieking off upstairs, and left McTavish to give Esme a full hour on the importance of routine, the especial danger of drink in cases like that of Terence, and the effect of 'the literatures of the cultures' on anti-social people.

After that they all went to Heathrow to see Mrs Fairweather off.

The Valleys still had the officious management of all the least important baggage, but Esme (whom Dr McTavish had told Sandra was attentive, appreciative, intelligent and thoroughly reliable) was put in charge of three large and important suitcases. Mrs Valley gave him a look that would have stopped a rhinoceros. Terence bought a bundle of horror tales at the bookstore and gave them to McTavish to carry. Mrs Fairweather went to ring the secretary up about some special cleansing tissues she had ordered at a well-known chemist's.

She came back in a state.

'Esme,' she screamed, 'Esme, that diabolical Chaser woman has made a muddle with my cleansing tissues. Now go, the moment you leave here, to Fiddle & Dig on Bond Street and tell them I do not – *not* – NOT want Curivalve – Curivalve, got it? – but the stuff I have specially sent – which is called Cosmoclite – COSMOCLITE,' she yelled through the entire building.

Cosmoclite and suchlike were Mrs Valley's department. She crumpled up as though she had been embraced by an ape.

'Perhaps, Sandra,' she suggested, 'I'd manage bett—'

'Got it, Esme?' said Sandra as though Mrs Valley were too drunk to be noticed.

'I've got it,' said Esme, with a smirk that went right through Mrs Valley's nervous system, 'anything else?'

'I – Whatever are these, Dr McTavish?' She seized the bumper-crop of horror tales.

'A diplomatic concession, Mrs Fairweather,' said the poor booby.

Sandra hurled them through a door marked private. Terence went pale.

'Clowns,' she said, 'surrounded by a circus of clowns.' She kissed Terence, pecked at Mrs Valley, looked at the three men with revulsion and vanished.

It had been a tiring day, so Dr McTavish took Esme and Terence to the most expensive restaurant he knew about and charged it to the Fairweather account. Mercifully he was too busy eating and drinking to say very much.

Later on the two of them set out for home in the garden van. Terence was exhausted, and so grieved by the loss of his literature that he remained absolutely silent. As he drove Esme assessed the situation.

Now in any other circumstances he would have been beside himself with rage at McTavish's interference with the prospects of Biarritz. As it was, he was not displeased. For all it now meant was that things would remain unsettled for a considerable time – and give him a chance to locate Uncle Bill Gomery. To achieve this he had, for a start, seven clear days without interference or commitment, and a passable garden van. He also had the house to himself. Breakfast, he had decided, would be at ten, while the rest of the day could be devoted to a comfortable neglect of routine and the search for Uncle Bill. In the evening they could drive into Cambridge or Ely to see the latest American pictures. This would bribe Terence into acquiescence as to how they spent the rest of the day – American films were now under an inviolable interdict – and would insure that he went to bed too late to wake up and disturb Esme in the morning.

And there was better yet. Since no one yet knew where they were later to go, there was a possible chance that he might be able to put his own word in when Sandra returned. McTavish and Aldeburgh he reckoned, with a little skill, to be able to discount (he would turn informer about the doctor's prodigality at Sandra's expense in the matter of dinner). This meant that if only he could discover where Uncle Bill was before Sandra came back, he might be able to arrange for them to go to the same place. It was a big if and a big might. But it was a possibility.

There was, however, one unknown element to be dealt with – Dr Fibula Trito. For Trito, it seemed, could be expected the following Saturday. In the first place this meant tidying things up and preparing a distinct impression of efficiency. At the same time Bellamy was coming from Eton for the week-end, so the atmosphere could have a considerable touch of cordiality, that 'home for the holidays' feeling, which would explain any latitude allowed and, he hoped, present himself in the light of a kindly but observant elder brother, whose acute understanding of the situation was suitably cloaked by a mask of jollity.

The thing was, what line was Trito going to take about Aldeburgh, routine and English pastime? Or about Biarritz? It seemed that the man was away for the time being, because otherwise he would have assumed immediate control. McTavish was merely second string. What Trito said went. He was a very vital figure indeed. In fact it was through him that one must really try to gain one's ends. Get him to adopt one's proposals as his own, and there one was. But again, if McTavish was only second string, he was a second string of Trito's recommendation. So much had been made obvious at dinner, when McTavish had referred (between courses) to a long-standing friendship and a high level of mutual esteem. It was therefore highly probable that Trito would merely adopt McTavish's suggestions. Of course, it might turn out that these were what one wanted, but somehow it seemed unlikely that American Uncle Bill would skulk away at Aldeburgh for the summer. On these points he must reserve judgment, he supposed, till he knew more of Uncle Bill and had met Dr Trito.

Then there was the question of Bellamy. Sandra had said that she did not want the two boys long together – Terence was a bad influence on his brother. A separate tutor was being engaged, and would appear at the beginning of August when Eton finally broke up. In point of fact this was not very far away : Long Leave from Eton this year was happening only a fortnight before the end of the half – due to the lateness in date of the match at Lord's. So what happened when Bellamy came home for good? His mother, having had (in theory at least) three weeks and more of Terence, would spend some time with the brother. Where Bellamy was, Terence wasn't to be. Therefore Terence and Esme would be free of Sandra. Come what may, this could only be regarded as a blessing, and of course it guaranteed unhampered action. But a lot – perhaps everything – depended on where in fact they were sent.

After a review of the occasions when he himself had returned from school, Esme decided that Sandra would probably want Bellamy to come first to Badlock, where his heavier belongings could be dumped and his clothes and person inspected. What it amounted to then was that on her return from Canada, just after Bellamy's Long Leave, she would have a clear ten days or more in which to decide on somewhere away from Badlock where Terence and himself might be sent so as to keep the boys apart. She would also have Trito's report. The more one looked at it the more seemed to depend on Dr Fibula Trito. One thing he could do was to make sure that Trito's report of the week-end confirmed the necessity for Terence to be kept away from Bellamy. With any luck they would have a fight – it should be easy enough to arrange: but in any event opinion seemed to run so strongly on this matter that it would be quite sufficient merely for himself to say how difficult it was to control them when they were together. He must also think, he supposed, of intelligent remarks to make to Dr Trito – something to impress him with his competence. . . . A dichotomy, that would do, a dichotomy in Terence's character. 'I have observed, Doctor, that one minute he will talk very intelligently on adult subjects, and that the next he will disappear to look at comic papers.' And then there was 'identification'. 'He identifies himself with characters of fiction or the cinema – not for ten minutes or so, but for hours, if not days, at a time. The character's world becomes his world. . . .' And that should suffice for a start. He must remember to make a list. What he would like to know, since a lot depended on it, was just how much influence Trito carried. It rather looked as if Sandra paid her psychiatrists a lot of money and very little attention – at any rate if their suggestions conflicted with her own. Report had it that Trito had been with her a long time and was the only person who had really been able to manage her. But that might be because he agreed to almost anything she said. But again, it looked as though what McTavish – Christ, brake, there isn't room—

There wasn't. Fenland roads are very narrow and a three-ton lorry had come round a corner only fifty yards in front. Both Esme and the lorry were driving inattentively, neither slowed down, they scraped in passing, and the back-door frame of the van was badly battered while half the top section of the doorpost was torn away. Terence woke up with a start, and they got out into the twilight road.

The fault was evenly divided. There was no occasion for fuss. They would say nothing whatever about it, a few pounds would settle the damage to the van. So eager was Esme to create an atmosphere of reconciliation that it never occurred to him that an insurance claim would require details of the other party involved. They drove on to Badlock to show their work to the gardener.

The gardener said it was not a bit serious, and would take twenty-odd pounds to repair. He would notify the agent, who in turn would notify the lawyer and the insurance company. Of course Mr Sa Foy had the name and address of the lorry-driver . . .? Well then, did he have the number of the lorry . . .? Well then, it looked as though twenty quid was coming out of Mrs Fairweather's pocket.

# VIII

This was a depressing thing to have occurred, but Esme didn't think much about it. After all, from what he could see of things, Sandra was involved in one crash after another : and all she did was merely to buy a bigger and faster car each time, so that the accident rate went up in geometrical proportion. A few pounds on a garden van were neither here nor there. Once more, Esme's lack of acquaintance with the rich was letting him down : when Sandra crashed a car, Sandra got the kick – both out of the crash and the next car. She paid without a murmur. But when Esme had a smash, though the money involved was by comparison nothing at all, it wasn't the same thing. She hadn't been there : money in excess of the bare necessary amount had been wasted : *ergo* she was being exploited. Another simple syllogism – with a general application that all young men involved with rich families would do well to bear in mind. While the rich can *see* their money being spent, no matter how foolishly spent, they are perfectly, indeed childishly, happy : provided they themselves are present, you can even spend it for them; but they grudge every sheet of lavatory paper used in their absence – which is tantamount to saying they grudge every sheet of lavatory paper that is used at all.

Esme, however, had yet to find this out, and in any event something occurred on the following Wednesday, something both miraculous and yet in a way irritating, that put the whole business of the garden van clean out of his head.

At eleven o'clock in the morning he went to talk to Terence, who, with more than usual disregard of routine, was lying in bed reading. Spread over the bed and the floor were the fruits of their expedition to Merlin's Bookstore in St Martin's Lane; Esme sat down on the end of the bed, and out of sheer idleness grabbed the first paper within range, which happened, of all things, to be the so-called 'Luritania Supplement' of the *New York Herald Tribune*.

This abominable rag filled him with disgust but at the same time a peculiar fascination. The *Luritania*, it seemed, was a new ocean-going liner of unsurpassed tonnage and amentities, and had made its maiden voyage from New York to Cherbourg some three weeks back. Nothing could be more 'regal' than the state apartments (photos on page 6 of this supplement), the dining-room was a sort of fairy palace, and the ballroom (chandeliers by Charue) had a floor you could see yourself dance in. There were also five different bars, six squash-courts, and a masseur's parlour for both sexes. The food, Esme learnt, was prepared so hygienically that a qualified doctor was employed whose sole job it was to detect possible contamination in the kitchens. Cartier, Molyneux, Balmain – a dozen other top names in jewels, clothes and furs – all had experienced and courteous representatives on board. On the *Luritania* one wanted for nothing except manna – and even that could doubtless be arranged.

There were also a few passengers. These ranged from a well-known Argentine diplomat down to Monsieur Yaw and a gang of students, who had been doing valuable field work as a representative party of the European League for T.W.E. (Teach the Workers Economics). Some of the passengers had little columns about themselves : the Princess Fuina Gheika (fresh from a drink cure in Boston, Mass.) was off to Cannes, Esme noted, to earn the right to another one; Guy Bolton, Jnr, had recovered from his nervous disorders consequent on failing his B.A. (Ord.) for the third time running, and was returning to Oxford for a fifth year of gas-fires and benzedrine; Mr Richard Temple Muir, who had just completed a tour round the world with his friend, Mr Peter Dixon, was joining his mother and the remnants of his capital in London; and Mr William Gomery, the poet and novelist, ——
Mr William Gomery, the poet and novelist, was going to spend a fortnight in Paris at the Bellman Hotel, from where he intended to fly to Bordeaux. There he would stay with friends and revise his latest book (*Ten Dahlias in a Window Box*) which was to be published the following spring. He was going to Biarritz in early August, where he had many friends, including the Duke and Duchess of Panton, who were also expected at the Hôtel du Palais.

'Hey, Terence,' he yelled before he could stop himself, 'I've found your Uncle Bill.'

'There's no call to scream about it,' said Terence, 'what do you mean, found him?'

'In the "Luritania Supplement". It says he's gone to Bordeaux to revise a novel called *Ten Dahlias in a Window Box.*'

'Crappy name,' said Terence.

'I didn't know he wrote novels.'

'Why should you? He doesn't so's anyone'd notice. He never sold ten thousand in his life.'

'He's going to Biarritz in August, to see the Duke and Duchess of Panton.'

'That means we'll be there,' said Terence, 'the Duke was sweet on Mother and she goes for Dukes.'

'Fair enough,' said Esme, and returned to Charue's photogenic chandeliers.

But a little consideration told him it was not as fair as all that.

For one thing, the odds against Terence and himself getting to Biarritz had considerably lengthened. Everybody seemed to frown whenever the place was mentioned. (He remembered Mrs Valley's tart remarks on the subject of poor 'Charles'.) Then there was the McTavish veto: and for all he knew it would be echoed, for the same or different reasons, by Dr Fibula Trito. Admittedly Sandra seemed fairly keen on going there, and no doubt the Duke who had been sweet on her (not to mention Uncle Bill) would provide a further attraction; but she was under no obligation whatever to take Terence and himself along with her. Finally, there was the desperate uncertainty and lack of balance that seemed to predominate in all her arrangements. A day or two ago, when he himself didn't know where he wanted to go, this very uncertainty, with the scope it gave for desirable alterations, had seemed an altogether excellent thing. Now that he had a definite goal, he longed for a little precision.

Another thing that was puzzling him more and more was the strange omission of Bill Gomery from Mr Chynnon's list. At first he had thought that it was a mere slip: Gomery, after all, could have been a very slight acquaintance of Marshal Acre's who had come to know Sandra better as the years went on. But everything pointed against this. In the first place the man was Bellamy's godfather : and this implied a fair degree of intimacy with Sandra at the time of Bellamy's adoption – which was not, after all, so very much later than the decease of Marshal Acre. Again, William Gomery had now been revealed in the light of a man of letters – a feeble one, no doubt, but well enough known as such to command snob value of the calibre required by the 'Luritania Supplement'. And if it was a question of snob value (on which issue, after all, the whole affair was hinged), what was all this about the Duke and Duchess of Panton? Even if Gomery had only been Acre's office-boy one would have thought that his subsequent advance, if nothing more, would have earned him a place in Mr Chynnon's list. The conclusion one drew was that there was something highly peculiar either about Uncle Bill, or about Mr Chynnon's list – if not both.

Here was a distinctly unsettling line of thought. For if you came to think of it, Mr Chynnon's list *was* a highly arbitrary document. Hotel guests and American friends – well and good. But why no one else? Both Sandra and Marshal Acre had travelled very widely, Sandra at least had a substantial place – still did – in the 'Continental set', and it was to be presumed they both had many friends littered all over the Continent, of whom not a few would have been seen frequently in America and almost certainly at Sandra's home on Long Island during and before the Acre courtship. Not to mention Sandra's friends in England.

The multiplicity of questions one could raise on the assumption that Mr Chynnon was playing double was quite beyond Esme's computation. The thing became a hideous and nightmarish matrix. Suppose, for example, you said that there was an Acre secret worth discovering but Mr Chynnon, for some reason of his own, wanted someone else to discover it : why, then, had he specifically directed one's attention that way, thus paying one for efforts that could have been more valuably employed in other directions and at the same time running a distinct, if minor risk of one's finding the secret after all? Why, for the matter of that, had he bothered to employ one at all? Granted the money meant nothing to him, the fact remained that he had taken the trouble to make complicated enquiries about oneself and one's past, and had been prepared to run the considerable risk of one's going to the police and having him charged for maleficent activities. Was one then a decoy? And, if so, whom was one decoying and whither? Or, to go back to the old hypothesis, was the omission of Gomery merely a clerical error after all? And the apparently arbitrary nature of the list merely a turn of one's imagination or the too rigid application of logic?

Esme, who by this time saw that if he was not to be involved in a revel-rout of interrogation he must be content to have a little patience, came to two comparatively sane decisions.

The first was that, since Mr Chynnon was now due for the first of his weekly reports he had better have it – and that it would tell him absolutely nothing. He accordingly sat down and told Dear Mr Chynnon that he was settling in, keeping his eyes skinned, and was sincerely E. S. Sa Foy.

The second may more properly be called a deduction, and was simply this: that whatever mystery there was about Marshal Acre, whatever was peculiar about William Gomery, and whatever might be the motives of Mr Chynnon, the answer lay with Uncle Bill, alias Bellamy's godfather, alias Sandra's torchbearer, alias the friend of the Duke of Panton, i.e. with William Gomery Esquire, poet and novelist, at present in Bordeaux and shortly to be in Biarritz. It was to Biarritz he must go to compete for the thousand pounds, if indeed the offer was genuine: as he had nothing else to do, he might as well assume it was; and it was therefore to Biarritz he must go. And there for the time being he must let the matter rest.

# IX

But there were a good many other things to occupy his attention. On the evening of the 'Luritania Supplement' discovery, Esme and Terence drove into Cambridge to see a film. Coming out they met a friend of Esme's who was up for the Long Vacation Term, and whose hospitality detained them till one in the morning. When they got back to Badlock they left a little note asking for breakfast at eleven o'clock. As they had both ingratiated themselves with the staff, and as on the whole they gave very little trouble, there was no reason to suppose anyone would mind very much.

Nobody did, and they were left to sleep in peace – or they would have been, had not that morning been selected for a series of 'phone calls by apparently everyone in the world that knew them.

The first was from the secretary in London and happened at ten o'clock. The boys were still in bed, said the maid, but she would fetch Mr Sa Foy.

'Still in bed, Mr Sa Foy?' said an icy voice.

'Yes,' said Esme awkwardly, 'that is, we've only just got up.'

'Well the thing is this,' said the secretary: 'we've just heard through the agent that you've had an accident. Is that the case?'

'Only a very small accident,' said Esme.

'I dare say, but Mr Gower, the lawyer, is very upset you haven't let him know about it. And there's another thing – you didn't get the name or anything of the other party, and the insurance have said they won't pay up.'

'I'm afraid so,' said Esme feebly.

'Well, everyone's very annoyed and thinks you've behaved in a thoroughly irresponsible way,' said Mrs Chaser with relish: 'and I really must say, Mr Sa Foy –'

'Is there anything you want doing?' The wind was whistling through Esme's pyjamas and he was beginning to feel curt.

'Yes: an accident report will be coming for you to fill in just in case the insurance will do anything. Have you reported the accident to the police?'

'Not yet,' said the miserable Esme.

'Well, it's meant to be done within twenty-four hours, so you'll have to be rather quick,' said Mrs Chaser sarcastically, and rang off with venom. Esme went back to bed to think it all over.

But not for long. At 10.30 the phone rang again. It was Mrs Valley. Mr Sa Foy was in bed but the maid would get him.

'Still in bed, Mr Sa Foy?' said Mrs Valley cuttingly.

'We've just started breakfast,' said Esme.

'The maid said you were in bed, still that's your business – I hear you've had an accident.'

Really, it might be a conspiracy.

'A very minor one,' said Esme.

'I don't know about that, but Mr Gower's absolutely furious, and says you've behaved in an irr—'

'I know he says that,' said Esme, 'what is it you want?'

'Well, since you ask, I rang up to tell you what time Bellamy's arriving. I 'phoned his house-master yesterday.' Interfering bitch.

'Well, what time is he arriving?'

'Friday evening, by the last train. He's going to Arundel first to play – '

'Thank you,' said Esme, taking his chance to ring off with a slam.

He just had time to get upstairs before Dr McTavish rang up. The maid appeared for the third time.

'Still in bed, Mr Sa Foy?' said McTavish gloomily.

'Yes,' said Esme, 'if you want to know, neither of us are feeling very well.'

'I'm sorry to hear that. You know how to get on to the local man all right?'

'Yes,' said Esme desperately, 'but I don't think that'll be necessary.'

'Well, don't take any risks with Terence. I hear you've had an accident.' Had the whole of London heard of it?

'Not really an accident, we only – '

'That may be, but Mr Gower is very anxious, I understand. I think perhaps you'd better – '

'I'm terribly sorry, Doctor,' said Esme, 'but Terence is calling upstairs. Is there anything in particular?'

'There is, in point of fact. Dr Trito has asked me to let you know he'll be arriving in time for lunch on Sunday. So have everything ready. Bellamy's going to be there too, they tell me.'

'Yes.'

'Well, if you find it hard to manage – if there's any sort of trouble – you know where to get me. Are you quite sure you wouldn't like me to ring the local man and have him come to see you and Terence, if you're not feeling very well?'

'No, please don't give yourself any trouble, Doctor,' Esme implored, 'he's just a little tired, that's all it is. I think I should get upstairs to him. It was so kind of you to ring up. Good – '

'Oh, one more thing,' said the inexorable McTavish, 'how's the routine going?'

'Magnificently,' said the hysterical Esme, 'athletic activity in the morning, an hour of cultural repose after lunch, further athletic activity till tea-time, and creative endeavour after dinner.'

'Good,' said McTavish dubiously, 'it's essential his hours should be regular and early and that there should be no drifting about. Good-bye, Mr Sa Foy.'

'Good-bye,' said Esme, and went clammily off to shave.

All this was upsetting enough, but there was nothing much to be done except wait for the insurance form and the return of Mrs Fairweather. Esme still didn't believe that anyone as rich as Sandra would make a fuss about the doorpost of a miserable garden van.

The next thing to be settled was a scheme for the approaching week-end. On the whole it seemed likely that this would settle itself, and Esme was confirmed in this view by his first meeting with Bellamy on Friday night.

The only things you noticed about Bellamy were his extreme size, his extreme niceness, his excellent sense of humour – and his entire lack of intelligence. No one was more conscious of this deficiency than himself, and he had wisely decided at an early age that he was not going to waste time and energy trying to develop what he hadn't got. This decision had apparently left plenty of time for the development of what he had got, so that his size, his niceness and his humour had come along better than ever. (All of which infuriated Sandra, for she, like all his schoolmasters, refused to understand that knowledge is only a waste of time if you don't get any fun out of it.) Bellamy, then, would really make no difference to anything at all. He was just something pleasant to have around.

Both boys seemed to know about Sandra's determination to keep them apart; and Esme rather meanly took advantage of this to hold a preliminary council as to the best way of impressing Trito.

'If you two want to see much of each other,' he said, 'we shall have to create a favourable impression on Dr Trito. You know him and I don't. What's the form?'

The form, it seemed, was Trito's enormous fondness for food, drink, comfort and backgammon. He always brought a backgammon board with him, and played on the system of optional doubling on a penny basis after each move, so that if you didn't watch out you lost a lot of money. Then he hated having things heavily organized for him – you just wanted to let him sit about in peace and make his own suggestions. Incidentally, he kept analysing everyone in the room the whole time he was there and whatever he was doing – whether for practice, for fun, or merely out of habit nobody knew. He was very nice about this, however, and never told you his conclusions unless, like Terence, it was you he had come to see.

All this sounded encouraging and simple. The cook was briefed with care and his room was seen to be warm and spotless. There was, however, a shortage of wine : for while there was enough gin on the sideboard to last a regiment for a week, the cellar was firmly locked and the key was thought to be with Sandra. This necessitated a drive to Sandra's wine-merchants in Ely, and a triumphant return with two bottles of champagne, a bottle of something white and light for Sunday lunch, and a superb bottle of claret over which Esme intended to launch any attack that might be necessary.

After this there was nothing to do except have a bottle of champagne to themselves on Saturday night and wait for Trito's arrival on the following day.

The great thing about Dr Fibula Trito was that, unlike pasteboard McTavish, he was made of flesh and blood.

He arrived in time for three large gins before lunch and complimented Esme upon the wine. He then went to sleep until tea-time, after which he cheerfully fleeced poor Bellamy of about a month's pocket-money before dinner. At dinner the two boys did the best thing one could ask and had a fight over who should keep the champagne cork. This meant that Esme would merely have disloyalty and not untruth as well upon his conscience when he told Dr Trito how difficult it was to manage them together. After dinner they disappeared to go on fighting somewhere else, Esme produced the claret, and Dr Trito, who had addressed about six words to Terence in the course of the whole day, began to get down to brass tacks.

'What do you think about all this?' he asked.

'I've hardly been here long enough to say,' began Esme cunningly : 'I think Terence is very nice and very intelligent, and I shall hope to be able to do something to help him find his feet.'

Dr Trito, who wore a made-up bow-tie and was very corpulent, began to look cynical.

'What sort of thing?' he asked in his purring voice.

'Well, keep him interested in pursuits and subjects that will be good for him and distract him from any sinister influence.'

'And that?' enquired Trito, pointing to a highly coloured copy of *Weird Tales* that had been carelessly left about.

'That,' said Esme, 'is just what I mean by a sinister influence. It's not so much the substance I deplore as the atrocious style. But I hope you'll agree with me that it's very important not to force him away openly from such things, but to try and steer him gradually in the right direction.'

'And what method do you propose using?' Trito had a smile which never left his face, but it was a variable smile, and expressed quite as much by the subtlety of its gradations as another man's face achieves by an entire change of expression. Like the moon, it had its phases. At the moment it was very new and very narrow.

'Yes, your method?' he insisted.

'Well,' said Esme, 'I had hoped that I should be able to discuss that with you. But I have drawn one or two elementary *inferences*, both from what Dr McTavish has told me and from my own *observations.*'

'I hear you've had an accident,' said Trito apropos of nothing at all.

'Yes, a lot of people seem to have heard that. It's absolutely nothing really.'

'I hear it will cost Sandra about twenty pounds.' He turned his smile full on. 'She'll hate that.'

'But surely – ' began Esme. Trito held up his hand, drained and refilled his glass in almost the same movement, and lit a cigarette.

'There's no but about it,' he said : 'now if you'll be so kind as to keep quiet I'll tell you a few things.' The smile had gone back to something like the Cheshire cat's. 'In the first place, I don't in the least want to hear about your "observations". I know them already. You were going to tell me about a "dichotomy" – you were going to use the very word – in Terence's character. (Don't be surprised, I've heard dozens of young men of your sort on the subject.) You were "going to point to a dichotomy" between his intelligence on the one hand and the vulgarity of his tastes on the other. You were then going to look very important, and say "Now what do I conclude from this?" After that there were going to be some commonplace remarks on the subject of slight concessions but an overall and beneficial control. You would have finished up by blinking your great eyes at me and asking my advice – to which you would have not listened because you would have been too busy thinking about the next intelligent remark you were going to make. So much,' he said very deliberately but with a very friendly look, 'for your "observations".

'The next thing we ought to get straight is that you know and I know that your salary is just so much money down the drain. Don't be alarmed, that's just a general observation about all private tutors. In your case,' he went on, 'it is more money than usual, but it's going down, if I may say so, a more than usually satisfactory drain. For while you are conceited, idle and unscrupulous, you have a small knowledge of literature and a genuine, if untutored, taste for wine.'

He paused to look almost sentimentally at the bottle.

'Now what, you may ask, has all this got to do with Terence? Well, I want you to understand from the beginning that whatever's wrong with Terence and whatever's going to be done about it, is entirely my affair. It's not your business to observe dichotomies, draw inferences, form conclusions or make pert remarks. All right?'

Esme nodded.

'His cure then, which,' said Trito with some satisfaction, 'will take a very long time, is for me to bother about. Now although whatever you do will almost certainly result in putting that cure back indefinitely, one thing is obvious. The more you're actually enjoying yourself, the more you're allowed to go to congenial places and do congenial things, the less bad temper and laziness you'll show. You might even,' he said a little wearily, 'become a stimulating companion. Now what did Dr McTavish suggest?'

'Athletic activity – sailing at Aldeburgh.'

'Sandra is one of the few rich women in England,' said Trito hopelessly, 'and McTavish suggests sailing. Followed up, I suppose, by a fortnight at the Edinburgh Festival.'

'Not exactly,' said Esme, 'though he did talk a lot about culture.'

'He's got culture on the brain,' said Trito, 'he talks about nothing else, and would probably tell you that Ulysses came from Dublin. And has Sandra made any suggestions?'

'She got as far as talking about Biarritz.'

'I thought I told you not to be pert. Now in Biarritz you have something more suitable to her income-group. I must say I'm rather taken with the idea. It would amuse you, you might therefore amuse Terence, and he'd have plenty to look at and think about. What's going to happen is all the old business about keeping Terence away from Bellamy, which I think can be allowed to pass muster as usual. Biarritz isn't really Bellamy's cup of tea, and in any case,' he said, 'we don't want the whole place cluttered up with private tutors. Bellamy can go and crawl after deer in Scotland – he'll love that and it'll do his figure good. Now let me think.'

In a fit of absent-mindedness he emptied the claret bottle into his glass and sat back looking at the ceiling.

'It'll work like this,' he said: 'when Sandra gets back I shall tell her that you and Terence must be out of the way before Eton breaks up. I shall suggest that she sends you to Dieppe with a car, and tells you to motor down to the south-west by slow degrees. She can join you in Biarritz – with myself, since I shall be anxious to assess the result of this experiment. The idea being that colour, excitement, movement and independence are just what Terence requires.'

'Dr McTavish was talking about stability, discipline, routine and early hours.'

'Dr McTavish,' said Trito, 'would be better occupied counting the remaining hairs on his head— No,' he said, 'one can't be as disloyal as that. Dr McTavish has made a mild error in his diagnosis. After some thought I have decided that the merits of his plan reside in its static nature. But while he is giving Terence no opportunity to deteriorate, he is likewise giving him no chance to progress. I am prepared to make a slight gamble in the interests of a possible and very favourable development. What do you think of the plan?'

'I think it's heaven. But if you don't mind my asking, is it certain that Mrs Fairweather will accept it?'

'I was coming to that. I can't, I'm afraid, give an absolute guarantee. On the one hand, I have considerable influence with her, having been her doctor and the boy's for several years. On the other hand there are a lot of elements one can't always control. To start with, she's so erratic that it has been said of her, "God proposes, Sandra disposes." For another thing, she pays a good deal of attention to two malicious women – her secretary and Mrs Valley – who are always with her. They've got nothing much against me, but they just don't like to see people like you and Terence enjoying themselves. There's been a lot of joy killed by those two.

'Then there's the question of expense. Whenever Sandra's not there, everything's meant to be on the cheap. Since she's never tried it herself, she's got the idea that "on the cheap", even nowadays, can mean something like five pence a day. You'd be all right *with her* in Biarritz, but what you'd be allowed for travelling through France would probably provide for a succession of nights in doss-houses. I'm always having trouble about that myself. Last time I went to Switzerland, she'd convinced herself she was so short of Swiss francs that I couldn't stay in the best hotels. I had to tell her that it was one thing being a student and hitch-hiking over Europe and quite another being a medical practitioner on business. Eventually I took the best room at each place I stopped just to teach her a lesson. You see the kind of thing we're up against.'

Esme did – and wished he had Trito's way of dealing with it.

'It's just possible too that she may take sufficient notice of

McTavish, whom she seems to like, to allow his ideas at any rate to keep you off the Continent if not to condemn you to Aldeburgh. There's a polite fiction going that McTavish and I co-operate, as I recommended him. As a matter of fact I recommended him because he promised he'd keep his mouth shut and string along with me. This is what comes of going away for a fortnight – people get ideas – McTavish of all people.

'Still, we'll do the best we can. And now,' he said succulently, 'it's time for a little backgammon.'

# X

After a good deal of havering about, it was decided that Esme and Terence should drive Bellamy back to Eton on Monday and then spend the night in London to meet Sandra off her 'plane the next day. For some reason it was thought she'd be glad to see them.

On the way down to Eton they discussed the prospects.

'Trito,' said Esme, 'seems very keen on your mother's idea of going to Biarritz. He wants us to drive slowly through France first.'

'Will I be coming?' said Bellamy, who had taken a great fancy to Esme, because here at last was someone about who liked his size and his giggling and sincerely condoned his lack of intelligence.

'I don't know about that,' said Esme rather guiltily, 'it depends on what Trito tells your mother. He seemed still to be harking on this business of keeping you two apart. That champagne cork . . .'

'I know,' said Bellamy sadly, 'they always say something like that. Then Terence goes somewhere nice and I'm sent off to Scotland. They seem to think I like Scotland.'

'Don't you?'

'Not a bit. It's damp and cold and uncomfortable, and everyone arranges for me to do the dampest, coldest and most uncomfortable things you can do.'

'Like what?'

'Like deer-stalking, for instance. Someone writes to Mother and says they've got three moth-eaten deer in a horrible park, and does she know anyone who wants to spend a week in their beastly castle and go stalking. "Just the thing for Bellamy," she says. I've even started intercepting the post and tearing up all letters from Scotland. Somehow I seem to get invited more than ever,' he concluded wistfully.

'Well, I shouldn't bother at the moment,' said Esme, 'there's a lot of things can happen in a few days. Trito was saying that Mrs Chaser and Mrs Valley would do their best to bitch everybody up.'

'They will at that,' said Terence, 'they'll both be getting their little tales ready about what went on when she was away. "Car smashes," they'll tell her, "in bed all the morning, rudeness on the telephone," everything they can think up.'

'Yes, we've been a little unlucky.'

Gloom descended on the garden van. (It was still unmended, as people seemed to nurse a forlorn hope about the insurance and said the 'man' would want to see it.)

'Of course, come to that,' said Terence, 'Trito seems to be acting rather odd. He's all for Mother getting rid of her cash, but it's generally slick little holidays for her with him tagging along as a kind of nanny. I get dumped in Ireland – Glengariff or some bloody place.'

Bellamy giggled.

'I s'pose the thing is,' Terence went on, 'that there's nothing much wrong with her any more, so now I've got to be the excuse for him to get a bit of sunshine.'

'She doesn't eat very much,' said Esme inanely.

'You're telling us. She lubricates her nerves with a bit of gin and steams along on that.'

'What about Mc Tavish?' asked Esme.

'He just hangs around when Trito's away. She seems to like him though. But you want to see her with Trito – Fibula darling this and Fibula darling that. He just purrs.'

'Then won't she take his suggestion?'

'Could be. But she likes to put her own spoke in, and he doesn't want to get in bad books with her.'

And that seemed to be about the sum of it. When they were nearing Eton, Bellamy disconcerted them all by starting to cry. Esme, who was always instantly melted by tears, gave him back the two pounds Trito had won off him. That only made him cry more. However, as Terence explained on the way back to London, there was nothing to worry about because Bellamy was so soft he cried whenever he left anyone he'd been with for more than a day. He even used to cry in the train coming home from school : when he left the castles in Scotland he hated so much he went into floods of tears; and when he'd left America he'd cried the whole twelve hours they were in the 'plane. You had to be very careful when Bellamy was going away, that was all. After dinner they went to the latest American film. Esme had an idea that he was going to need all the help Terence could give him.

There was something in that. Next morning everyone in London seemed to descend on 6, St Ambrose Gate – like flies on a rotten plum. Sandra was due about tea-time; but well before twelve the whole house was full to bursting. The secretary arrived at nine-thirty, followed closely by the two Valleys. About eleven o'clock McTavish arrived – in the vanguard of a screaming mob of Sandra's aunts, friends, hangers-on and general dependants, all of whom grabbed at Terence in concert and nearly tore him apart. Last of all appeared Trito, who treated Esme to an enormous wink and made straight for a tray of drinks.

They all settled happily down to discuss the probable pickings to be gleaned from Sandra's latest expedition, while some, like the Valleys, busied themselves with little jobs, such as ringing up to see if the 'plane would be on time, poking their noses into Sandra's bedroom to make sure the bed had been made up and so on. The whole place buzzed with activity and anticipation, and no one showed the slightest signs of going away to have lunch – except, of course, for Trito (McTavish, as Terence had predicted, just stood around) who whisked the two boys off to somewhere he knew of in Jermyn Street and managed to get them four pounds worth of food and drink on Sandra's account there.

'We shall need all our strength,' he explained.

When they returned to St Ambrose Gate, the crowd was even thicker and the excitement was mounting rapidly. On the whole Esme rather enjoyed it, but he noticed that he himself was receiving a quantity of hostile looks all round, particularly from the Valleys and Mrs Chaser, and that the word Biarritz, accompanied by vigorous head-shakings, was all over the house. Trito got looks in which respect, ingratiation and jealousy were subtly blended, while Terence had already picked up three pounds in tips and was busy patrolling from one group to another. Eventually Esme decided that the atmosphere was so unhealthy that they went out for half an hour to buy American ties with the three pounds.

It had been arranged that a priority group, consisting of Terence, Esme, the two Valleys and Dr Trito, should go to

Northolt in the powder-blue Rolls. The main party would wait behind ready to seize on Sandra's luggage the instant she arrived. Esme received more hostile looks than ever when he got into the Rolls with Terence.

For some unaccountable reason the 'plane was half-an-hour early, and Sandra was storming with rage when they met her.

'I've got presents for you all,' she screamed, and threw a series of small packages at them in rapid succession : 'now for Christ's sake let's get out.'

This wasn't as easy as it sounded, for her luggage had doubled itself during her absence. (The wretched lady's maid was nowhere to be seen, and must, thought Esme, have got lost in Canada.) But eventually they started at breakneck speed for London, Sandra yelling at them at the top of her voice about all the wonderful things she'd brought back.

'. . . a camera,' she roared, 'which develops its own photos. You take the picture, shut the camera, count a hundred, open it again at the back and there's the photo. How have things been?' she shrieked at Esme.

Esme was just opening his mouth to say that things had been lovely, but Mrs Valley saw her chance and was in before him.

'They've had trouble with the van,' she smirked.

Sandra's face went black.

'What sort of trouble?' she said icily.

'They've smashed a doorpost,' said Mrs Valley.

'Only part of a doorpost,' said Esme feebly.

There was a grim silence.

'Terence hasn't been very well,' said Mrs Valley.

'Did you have the doctor?'

'It was practically nothing,' said Esme.

'Well, Dr McTavish rang up,' said Mrs Valley, 'and Terence was in bed at eleven o'clock – so was Mr Sa Foy – so Dr McTavish said . . .'

Esme began to sweat.

'Terence was over-tired,' he said.

'I don't wonder,' said Mrs Valley, 'considering the time they used to get home at night. Once I rang up, as late as half past eleven, and Mary said . . .'

So that was it. What else had Mrs Valley found out? Plenty.

'How was Bellamy?' asked Sandra frigidly.

'He ought to be all right now,' said Mrs Valley, 'Mrs Chaser says she's just had the expense account, from Mr Sa Foy, and he's given Bellamy two pounds.'

'Who told you to give Bellamy two pounds?' screamed Sandra.

'Well, he was a bit upset when he went off, and hadn't got any money, and I thought...'

'I don't doubt you did. Now listen to me, Mr Sa Foy. When we get to St Ambrose Gate, you'll get into whatever you came to London in – a train, I hope – and go straight back to Badlock and stay there every minute of the day till you hear from me. It's quite obvious that the two of you are not to be trusted and I shall have to think what to do. I shall want to talk to you, Fibula, so stay around when we get there.'

Esme's blood froze. Biarritz, Mr Chynnon, Uncle Bill Gomery and his novels – all chased round his head on a frantic backcloth of hysteria against which loomed the figure of himself with two suitcases standing penniless on Badlock station. Everybody had gone very quiet indeed, and they drew up in St Ambrose Gate with a screech that must have taken a month's wear out of the tyres.

Then everything came to life again. Sandra disappeared into a screaming vortex of figures, her luggage was carried in triumph to her bedroom, everyone said how tired she must be – 'darling, but is that really for me?' – McTavish tried to get near her and was knocked down, the telephone rang unheeded, the bedroom filled up like a test-tube, a suitcase suffered the fate of Orpheus at the hands of the Bacchant women, Terence was sick in the lavatory (Trito's lunch and the excitement), and the Valleys went on one side to look at their presents.

Dr Trito took Esme into a corner.

'There's not the slightest need for worry,' he said. 'Get back to Badlock at once and I'll deal with Sandra. We caught her in a bad moment, but I'll fix her up with a tablet or something and talk to her when that Valley woman's out of the way. Just at the moment, though, the Biarritz outlook isn't so bright. Push off and leave her to me.'

Terence was still a bit green, but stood up to the departure manfully. Neither of them spoke till they were well past Letchworth.

Esme never really heard a full account of what happened in London after their departure. Some weeks later, however, Trito did say a little on the subject in passing, and what it added up to was horrific. Esme gathered that after the spoils had been divided and the less important hangers-on had gone, Mrs Valley and Mrs Chaser, along with a few aunts who were in the know, had got round Sandra in a circle and really let her have it on the subject of Esme Sa Foy. He had been accused of every kind of irregularity, the charges ranging from criminal neglect of Terence's health, safety, and condition at one end of the scale, to having dirty finger-nails at the other. His carelessness over the car made a big point, undue fondness for his bed (with a hint at undue fondness for the bottle) made another. At this stage, it seemed, Trito had cleared them all out, produced a soothing pill and given a very encouraging account of his week-end. Esme, he had pointed out, was not just another young man, he was highly intelligent, highly cultivated, and highly sensitive, all of which was very good for Terence, who was apt to be a bit coarse. He himself was satisfied – and after all he was the only person who had *been* to Badlock – that Esme's administration, while slightly on the indulgent side (and even here one must remember that he had to win Terence's confidence), was in every respect suitable. Sandra must not get worked up by a whole lot of tattling women.

He had then gone on to say how essential it was that the boys be kept apart – mentioning the fight but not the champagne cork. Sandra must have Terence well clear of Badlock by the date of Bellamy's return, and he would like to suggest the following plan. . . . Just as he was enlarging on its merits, the secretary had stumped in with a final and curt refusal to pay up from the insurance company, to be followed a moment later by McTavish, who had a black eye and seemed determined to make us much trouble as possible. McTavish had talked for half an hour about English activities, sailing, and relatives he apparently had in Aldeburgh who ran inexpensive private hotels. This was particularly irritating of McTavish as he was just off for a month's holiday and another few hours would have seen him out of the way.

At this juncture Sandra had behaved comparatively reasonably and decided on a compromise. Esme and Terence should be sent to Aldeburgh as soon as it could be arranged, partly as a punishment – she wasn't quite sure for what – partly to sail and play tennis, but mainly to keep them out of the way when Bellamy arrived. At Aldeburgh they must stay until she had inspected and despatched Bellamy and his tutor wherever (Scotland) she decided to send them. Meanwhile she would consider the whole question of Biarritz once more. She was doubtful about the motor tour after what had happened with the van. As for the expense of it all, it made her sick to think of it.

Whether Trito's account was substantially true, Esme never discovered. But in any event Sandra certainly appeared more or less calm at Badlock on the Friday after her arrival at Northolt, and announced that they could expect to proceed to Aldeburgh – by train – on the following Tuesday and for an indefinite period. There they would sail, play tennis, and stay in a private hotel McTavish had recommended. Other plans, she concluded, were under consideration.

So for the time being there was nothing for it but to look the trains out. Without exception they involved three changes and a picnic lunch.

# XI

It was rather a depressed couple which on Tuesday morning, complete with bathing-trunks, tennis-racquets and golf-clubs (a last minute thought of Sandra's) climbed into a first-class compartment at Badlock station. Sandra had given strict instructions they should travel third, but Esme proposed to make up the difference by economizing over the number of times they went sailing. Terence was in agreement with him about this. Indeed their attitudes to Aldeburgh harmonized very comfortably.

Intrinsically, Esme felt, being sent to Aldeburgh was one of the most disagreeable things that could happen. But when you considered the particular situation it wasn't quite so bad. They were moving firmly out of the Valleys' sphere of knowledge, and even McTavish's relative could hardly come up to the Valleys' standard of malice. More important than this, one had to remember that Uncle Bill Gomery was not expected in Biarritz till the first week in August. There was not much point in getting there till then – in fact it would be a disadvantage : there would be little chance of getting to Bordeaux and the francs allowed would have a big gap in them by the time he did arrive. Above all, he now felt that he had a firm and competent ally in Trito, who would hover between London and Badlock directing everything for the best.

But it didn't do to be too sanguine. Uncle Bill might not be due in Biarritz till August, but that was now little more than a week away. One would need all the time one could get to work on Uncle Bill, so that it would be irritating to arrive just when he was starting to pack. There was the further possibility that if one just settled down to stagnate in Aldeburgh, one might be left there almost for ever. Bellamy would come and go, August would wear on and on . . . . It didn't really bear thinking about; but there was no doubt that if one side of Sandra's nature expressed itself by uprooting people without reason or warning, there was another side which sometimes just forgot about them entirely and left them wherever they were to rot. Once more, it was perfectly certain that the Valleys and Mrs Chaser wouldn't let any grass grow. They'd be busily working on Sandra whenever they saw a chance, doubtless extolling the suitability and healthy air of Aldeburgh and denying those qualities to Biarritz. Trito was there single-handed and presumably had a good deal else to attend to. One must give one's ally proper support.

It seemed to Esme that there was one obvious move that would see they were not forgotten, that would leave no one any time to listen to the Valleys – in short would force Sandra's hand so much that she might pack them off to France immediately. This was for them to be compelled to return to Badlock at almost the same time as Bellamy. How they were to get themselves compelled to return was another matter. But once assuming they did, with Trito plugging away at the absolute necessity of the boys being kept apart, the ensuing confusion would probably result in everyone being sent flying off in different directions like sparks from a Catherine wheel.

At first sight there was an obvious objection to this plan, but Esme didn't think it would stick. The objection was that the confusion might be so tremendous that they would indeed be sent flying off – to the first place Sandra thought of, which might be anywhere. This he countered by the reflexion that Trito would almost certainly be called in to assist, and that in any case Biarritz now seemed to be permanently on Sandra's mind. This was odd, since her mind was so diffuse. But over the week-end she had given the impression of having forgotten it was possible to send anyone anywhere except to Biarritz or Aldeburgh. It was a sort of fixation, and caused, he supposed, by the fact that everyone round her was constantly talking in terms of one or the other. But whatever the reason might be there it was. And this being the case, there was, as he had decided, only one thing to do : to set about achieving a specious return for Terence and himself on or before that next day week, on which date Bellamy returned for the summer holidays.

As for Mr Chynnon, he had sent him another report the preceding Wednesday and would repeat the performance tomorrow.

The last two had said nothing at all, neither would the third. He had received no sort of acknowledgement, and was indeed rather beginning to doubt if Mr Chynnon had ever existed. This would be put to the test in about a week's time, when the first of his cash instalments was due. Meanwhile the force of habit was strong and the pursuit of even a legendary thousand pounds was absorbing: there was no point in relaxing his efforts even if, at the moment, they consisted only of this rather dull and wearing business of intriguing, against the clock, for a passage to Biarritz.

Before he could start devising ways and means for a return he had to see what they had been let in for by McTavish.

It was pretty grim. Esme had had a letter from the secretary the day before, wishing them good weather with a sneer and instructing them, on arrival at Aldeburgh, to proceed to the Downs Private Hotel, Tennis Court Lane. There was only one redeeming feature about the place – namely that Sandra, who had taken no interest in the arrangements other than to give orders for them to be made, knew neither the address or the telephone number and therefore probably wouldn't ring up for at least twenty-four hours.

They reminded each other of this but their hearts sank. The Downs had every ingredient in a prescription for the most complete misery. It was unlicensed, it was spotlessly clean, it was full of family feeling. You couldn't order the servants about because they were part of the family; in fact they ordered you about if they harboured the slightest suspicion that you were out to be 'unhelpful', that is to say if you were so rash as to expect a tenth part of the convenience and comfort for which you paid, apparently, fifteen guineas a week. The food (which to do everyone justice, had always been excellent at Badlock) was as English as Sherwood Forest and as heavy as a cannon ball. Worst of all, routine prevailed. You must be out of bed by nine, because, even if you didn't want breakfast, the maids who did your room could on no account be inconvenienced. It was considered very odd if you were inside the house at all between ten and one – you were expected to be on the beach or sailing. Lunch, which was the heaviest and most English meal of the day, was rigidly at one, and the same unwritten embargo about not hanging around inside was in force until six o'clock. Then, if you felt strong enough to endure the multitude of printed prohibitions inside the bathroom and spoken ones outside it, you could have a bath in two inches of water and a raging draught.

After this there was a feeble pretence at gaiety. The Downs was unlicensed, but you could buy your own bottle of sherry by arrangement with Miss Loss, the proprietor, and at extortionate rates. This had your name written on it, and was then carefully hidden away, so that on no account could you get at it during the day, to be produced on a silver salver at quarter to seven sharp along with everybody else's. You then stood around in the lounge drinking it in minute glasses (it was, of course, not done to refill yourself more than once) and in the company of a miscellaneous variety of senior servants, like the housekeeper, who called you by your Christian name and waited to be given a drink. Much as you longed for your bottle, this was perhaps the worst feature of the day, since you were both frustrated and exploited more than at any other time.

After dinner you could go out – if you dared, and if you promised to be in by ten-thirty. There was in any case nothing to go out for except a sleazy cinema which even Terence rejected.

The great rule at the Downs was that everyone was a 'guest'. This meant that you had come by sole courtesy of Miss Clarence Loss (however much you might be paying) and that therefore there was due to herself, her servants, her house and her ideas the reverence and consideration that would be due to the Queen if you were staying at Windsor Castle. Miss Loss took her position as hostess very seriously. It was up to her, she felt, not only to discipline her guests but to organize them into appropriate amusements. As you were denied the anonymity of a hotel guest, it was a full-time job to evade her. At half past nine in the morning she appeared in full sail with suggestions, lists, addresses, and a string of local girls who had been sent up by anxious mothers to be dealt with by 'Clarie' Loss and parked on her male guests. 'Here's June,' Miss Loss would say, 'she can't wait to get in a sailing boat with you,' or, 'Jean's a demon on the tennis-court,' and so on. The girl in question would look at you with a hangdog, supplicating, hypnotizing look all over her stupid and spotty face, and it required all your presence of mind to remember you were 'fixed up' all that morning – and all that afternoon too.

Miss Loss was a cousin of Dr McTavish. She had therefore

been treated to a preliminary account of Terence which had made her intensely curious but not a little apprehensive. Esme was quick enough to spot this : he made a mental reservation that it might be useful shortly, and, for immediate purposes, took Miss Loss on one side and told her he would have to be very careful with Terence for a day or two, that they would move largely on their own, and that it would be some time before he wanted her to be so kind as to start making 'arrangements' and 'introductions'. Nothing, however, could stop her from giving him a list of people who would be prepared to hire out sailing boats and act as instructors on them. He had the good sense to accept the list gracefully, and withdrew, with a sinister but pitying look in the direction of Terence. This, he reckoned, would keep Miss Loss quiet for a bit.

On the whole it did. Fearful lest some unspecified eruption should occur, bringing with it scandal and decline of custom, Miss Loss left Terence and Esme very much to themselves. In view of the peculiar nature of the circumstances, they were even allowed a good deal of latitude in the matter of being 'unhelpful'. They showed, for example, a marked tendency to spend most of the day upstairs in their room. In the usual way this would have been considered a double violation of the rules laid down for guests at the Downs, in that not only were they in the house when every self-respecting person should have been out of it but they were also making extra work for the maids by preventing them getting into their bedroom and then, when they did go out, instantly making it untidy again on their return. Still, Miss Loss felt that it was perhaps the best place for them, ensuring, as it did, that any nameless disaster which might occur would at least occur in private. Esme, in fact, had succeeded in hedging them round with a privacy which was, for the Downs, phenomenal.

The days began to pass rather pleasantly. They would get reluctantly up at the specified time, but after breakfast would proceed about half-way back to bed again, lying under the counterpanes reading. This was a great joy to Esme who had had practically no time at all to read in the last three weeks. He had been thoughtful enough before starting to pack a minimum of athletic necessities and a maximum of books, and Terence had come with an enormous store of horror tales and space literature. He too was perfectly content. He had the most wonderful gift, Esme noticed with satisfaction, of doing absolutely nothing whatever with complete happiness and for hours on end. When this failed him, which was seldom, he would then read in a desultory way, draw a few unwholesome pictures, or play patience. Every now and again they had a friendly game of racing-demon. It was very pleasant. Here, Esme felt, was another instalment of his rest-cure, and he would be in perfect shape to deal with whatever next awaited them.

After lunch they used to feel a little restless, and in any case thought perhaps that an attempt at action would please Miss Loss, so they used to go 'sailing'. This meant a short and pleasant walk down to the estuary of the Alde, where they would admire the yachts.

'They look very pretty, anchored there like that,' Esme used to say.

'From this distance – yes,' said Terence firmly.

After that they used to walk back, and Terence would eat an enormous tea in Aldeburgh, while Esme entered their sailing trip on the expense account.

'A pound to hire of yacht for two hours,' he said, 'and ten shillings for the instructor. I think we shall know enough in a day or two to stop having an instructor.'

Terence, who was indebted to the instructor for ice-creams and cigarettes, wasn't sure on this point.

'I feel we have a lot to learn,' he said.

On one occasion they actually did play tennis to ease their consciences. This was a pity, because they both lost their tempers after the second game and Terence hit Esme with his tennis-racquet.

'After that we're certainly not going to try golf,' said Esme later.

As a matter of fact it was really a very good thing, because the incident was immediately reported to Miss Loss by someone who happened to have witnessed it, and she respected their privacy more than ever in consequence. (It was also to be a help later on when Esme conceived and carried out his plan.)

Apart from these strenuous excursions, Aldeburgh, in its way, was a very charming little place. The beach was shingly and nothing much happened on it, but the sea front was pleasant to walk along, and Esme found several nice little pubs where they would spend a long time in the mornings, and the evening. They even paid a visit to the cinema, which wasn't quite as sleazy as it looked. Then there were book shops and antique shops, an amusement arcade with slot-machines, a café with an orchestra, and once it was nearly warm enough to bathe. Altogether it was just the place to potter about in. Esme began to withdraw his initial hostility and would probably have settled down without any fuss had it not been for his increasing consciousness of time's winged chariot hurrying up behind him and Uncle Bill Gomery telling his friends in Bordeaux that it was time he pushed on to Biarritz. Aldeburgh was a soothing place, but he mustn't allow himself to be soothed. Something had to be done: and one afternoon he suddenly saw his way.

They were sitting in the conservatory after lunch talking to a family they had been so ill-advised as to become friendly with. It was really quite a nice family, however, and consisted of a sensible, Esther McCrackenish sort of woman with short, grey hair, her ineffective and once military husband, a son in the Rifle Brigade and a daughter in a repertory theatre. It was the Rifle Brigade tie that had started Esme off with the son, while the rest of the ménage had been introduced subsequently.

Now the daughter was rather an attractive girl who wore trousers, and for some reason found great favour with Terence, whom she used to encourage with bold looks and cigarettes. On this occasion the rest of the family drifted off to the beach and Esme drifted off to fetch a book, leaving the two of them alone. As he came back he took a look through a lounge window which faced straight into the conservatory, and was treated to a very charming spectacle.

The girl had heaved herself up full length on to a settee, raised her knees and was pretending to read a book. With her disengaged hand, however, she kept pulling one of her trouser-legs up, apparently in order to scratch herself, till by degrees it reached the knee and even an inch or two higher. When she couldn't get it any further she flicked it back and started the whole performance over again.

Now she was revealing far less than one could have been seen with ease at any hour on the beach; but something in her method, in the repetition of her movements, in the way she made them, endowed the exhibition with a lascivious significance Esme didn't fail to appreciate. As for Terence, he was sitting right forward on his chair, which was about two yards away, with his eyes nearly falling out of his head, his hands clasped, and his whole body absolutely rigid. He had better, decided Esme, be left there to get over it in his own time. And it was at this moment that he conceived his idea for escape.

There were two essentials for his plan. The first was that Terence should be seen about as much as possible with little Miss Moorsom who was the girl in question. This was easily arranged. Esme asked her and her family to have glasses of sherry, he took her out to a pub with Terence and left them in the lounge when they returned, and finally he gave Terence five shillings to take her out to the pictures. With a wink here and a nod there he soon converted the whole thing into a typical little boarding-house joke (adolescence, innocence, and sheep's eyes). Miss Loss was delighted – they were all one happy family party after all – and the girl's family, who had seen this sort of thing before, were pleasantly indifferent.

The next essential was taken care of by Esme on Sunday morning – a good time, he always found, for getting away with even the most transparent pieces of deceit. Terence, excused church, was playing patience.

'I've got a commission for you,' said Esme suddenly.

' ?'

'I want you to do a drawing for me. Five bob offered if it's what I'm after – it's rather a tricky bit of work. All to do with a joke I have with a friend of mine.'

'What sort of joke?'

'Well, it's about something that happened to him once which we haven't let him forget. He was with a girl he knew in her house and asked her to lend him some money or something. Quite unexpectedly she fainted. He didn't know what to do, but he had an idea she should be lain out flat. So he made a big effort and picked her up and put her on the hall table. But as she'd fallen on her face, he'd picked her up face downward and put her down on her stomach – the hall table was too small anyway, so her legs were just left dangling. And just when he was going to turn her over and start fanning her and throwing water about, her mother walked in through the front door. So there he was muddling around trying to turn this girl over and getting mixed up with her legs, when her mother marched in and found herself staring straight at her daughter's bottom. She didn't allow my friend to call again,' concluded Esme rather vaguely.

'What must I draw?'

'Well that's the point. I'd like a girl – dark hair for choice – sort of slung over a table. As I've told you, she's got to have rather a prominent behind – that's an important part of it, so I suggest you put her in trousers or something. In fact it's so tricky,' he went on hurriedly, 'that I'll offer seven-and-six. Half-a-crown in advance – catch.'

'I still don't get the joke,' said Terence, settling down to work.

It was now up to Esme to choose his moment. This must be done with care, for if his coup fell either too early or too late, Sandra might be able to take preventive action. Bellamy was due at Badlock by lunch-time on Wednesday. After furtively consulting Bradshaw – trains were rather important – he decided to strike on Wednesday morning.

'Clarie' Loss appeared with her lists and a pair of girls at about ten o'clock. But before she could introduce anyone, Esme had her on one side and said he must speak to her instantly – it was most urgent. So the girls were left in an even more embarrassing situation than usual – just standing around knowing no one – while Esme and Miss Loss (pleasantly agitated) vanished into her private sitting-room.

'Take a look at this,' said Esme, and thrust Terence's drawing at her.

Miss Loss nearly fell out of her seat.

'But really,' she said, 'I can't imagine – '

'I found it by Terence's bed this morning,' continued Esme sternly, 'do you know who it's of?'

'Well, I – '

'If you look at the colour of the hair and notice the emphasis on the trousers, you'll soon get there.'

'But surely – it can't – but they were such friends, Mr Sa Foy.'

'It's happened before,' said Esme grimly, and gave a swift and painful account of what happened to the gardener's boy.

'It's a melancholy trait in his character,' he went on, 'it's a twist given to ordinary affection by some violent and uncontrollable impulse at the root of his being.'

'But what will you do?'

'There's only one thing I can do,' said Esme, 'and that's to take him home. For his own sake, for your sake. Mind you, it might well mean, or at any rate lead to, nothing at all. That's a risk I can't take. I'm sorry about this, Miss Loss, we've been very happy and very comfortable. However, I'm sure you realize the difficulty of my position – if anything should . . . and your own position too.'

Miss Loss, who remembered the tennis-racquet incident, seemed to realize that.

'Very well then. Now if you'd be so good as to tell the other guests we've been called away suddenly, it would be a great help. I shall tell Terence merely that there's been an error on the part of Mrs Fairweather's secretary over the bookings, and that our rooms are required today. Also, I must ring up Mrs Fairweather and tell her what's occurred – no, it's very kind, Miss Loss, but I mustn't keep you, the 'phone in the box will do – it's quite private.'

He left the bewildered Miss Loss to shepherd off her girls, and hurried to the 'phone box. He managed to get through to Sandra's bedroom. She was distinctly disagreeable, having left instructions that she was on no account to be woken up.

'Yurse?' she said blurrily.

'Oh, Sandra, it's Esme here,' he said brightly, 'now look here : that dismal Loss woman has gone and made a muddle of her bookings – she only told me this morning, which was so helpful, but she says we'll have to get out today. I've tried a lot of other places, but it's slap in the middle of the season and they're all booked out. So I'm afraid we shall have to get on a train and come back.'

'Oh God,' said Sandra, 'is she quite sure? Springing it on me like this – it's so extraordinary. Look, Esme, get her on the 'phone will you, I'll have a stiff word with her and see what I can do.'

'Hang on,' said Esme. He collared Miss Loss on the lawn and brought her in.

'It's been rather a shock to Mrs Fairweather,' he said, 'so I'm sure you'll be very careful what you say and not mind if she seems a bit hasty.'

'Hullo,' said Miss Loss, 'Miss Loss.'

'Oh,' said Sandra like a lion, 'I've heard from Mr Sa Foy what's happened, Miss Loss, and that they'll have to come back. Is that the case?'

'Well,' said Miss Loss, 'I really think it might be best, don't you?'

'It's a bit too bad,' said Sandra, 'having people come to your hotel like this, when my secretary booked for a clear fortnight.'

'But I wasn't to know, was I?'

'Good heavens, woman, who else would if you don't? Well you can't keep 'em?'

'I'm afraid not, Mrs Fairweather.'

'And there's nowhere else they can go?'

'I don't think so, in the season. And even if there were –'

'Well that's that, I suppose. I'm very displeased, Miss Loss. I shall expect a discount on your bill for inconvenience caused. Now give me Mr Sa Foy, will you?'

'She seemed to blame poor Miss Moorson,' said Miss Loss later.

'Yes, she gets like that,' said Esme, 'it's the strain, poor woman. But there's no need to worry, Miss Loss : just send your account straight in to the secretary, and everything will be all right.'

Or that was what he hoped. Originally he had intended to take Terence's drawing back to Badlock and use the same excuse right through. This would have had the advantage of homogeneity; but if Miss Loss was a fool, Sandra wasn't. Besides, it would have been very unkind to Terence – nobody cared what Miss Loss thought, but Sandra was another matter, apart from what Trito would have said when he saw right through it all.

Even as things were, there were sufficient loose ends lying about. Heaven alone knew what Miss Loss would tell her cousin Dr McTavish. Mercifully he was away on his vacation, and even if he were to receive a letter and make enquiries, it would all take a very long time. Esme only hoped Miss Loss wouldn't enclose a chatty letter with her account. If she did, with any luck she'd only refer to the 'unfortunate thing which occurred', but you could never tell. He would have paid the account himself, despite the fact it would probably have taken a year to get the money out of Sandra, but his funds were sinking, he'd need as much as possible in Biarritz if they got there, and in any case it would have been thought a little odd all round.

No, there was a lot to worry about, but he could hardly have done much better. And whatever else, the immediate effect of it all should be excellent. Trains from Aldeburgh in the Badlock direction left only at 8.30 in the morning or shortly before lunch-time. They had had to take the lunch-time train, and would therefore reach Badlock far too late to be disposed of that night, in the event of anyone having that idea. Sandra would have heard from him much too late to do anything about Bellamy, who would have been sitting tearfully in the train from Eton when he rung her up. She might, of course, have bundled Bellamy away after lunch, but that did seem a little excessive. And even if she had, she would want Bellamy back, and lose no time in disposing of himself and Terence. Whichever way you looked at it, she had to do that within about a week. For either Bellamy was at Badlock, making Terence and himself *de trop*, or else Bellamy had been hurriedly parked out, but under so temporary an arrangement that she would have to get rid of them just the same. Either way she was trapped. And with any luck Trito would be there to give her suitable guidance in the predicament.

# XII

When they arrived at Badlock station Bellamy and Trito were there to meet them, Bellamy beaming all over his face and Trito wearing his slyest smile.

'So you didn't stay long at Aldeburgh?' he said.

'We couldn't,' said Esme.

'No, I don't suppose so. Well, there's a fine party gathered here for your reception.'

'Yes,' put in Bellamy, 'Mother's brought Mrs Chaser down, and the Valleys have been asked to see me. I wish they hadn't wanted to.'

'Well,' said Esme smugly, 'I suppose she'll have to think of somewhere else to send us now.'

'She was in a hopping rage when I arrived,' said Bellamy, 'she called Miss Loss everything she knew. Then she cheered up a bit.'

'Why?' asked Terence.

'Because Bellamy's just had a bit of luck,' said Trito meaningly.

'Yes,' said Bellamy sadly, 'a letter came this evening by express post saying the Lanchesters have suddenly got a vacancy for the twelfth. They've even asked me a few days earlier.'

'You ought to be jolly grateful,' said Terence with a giggle.

'Everyone thinks it's just the thing for Bellamy,' said Trito.

So no doubt it was, thought Esme savagely, but it was going to get Bellamy out of the way a damned sight too quickly.

'When are you going?' he asked.

'Night train on Saturday,' said Bellamy glumly, 'I've got a tutor coming tomorrow who's coming too.'

Esme's blood froze. That only left Thursday and Friday. Sandra would never object to them all being together for only two

120

days, which meant she could go on 'considering' for as long as she liked. She might even do so to such effect that she would snap out of her Biarritz fixation – especially with the Valleys around – and in any case valuable time was going to be lost.

'Sandra's very pleased about it,' said Trito, 'she says that now the house won't be overcrowded. Since she's got nothing to worry about, I'm going back to town tomorrow.'

Esme nearly choked. This was what came of such damned cleverness. You created very skilfully a highly promising situation – and then a letter came along and it just fizzled out. He'd stuck his neck out a long way and to no purpose whatever. Trito seemed to have divined his hopes and something of his dismay at what had occurred. When they reached the house he took him off for a quiet drink.

'Do cheer up,' he said, 'I'm doing my best, and she's sure to send you off when the mood takes her.'

'It's taking a long time to take her.'

'And Terence has got a long holiday.'

It was no good trying to explain how cold this bit of comfort was. Esme went to bed.

The next morning they took Trito to his train and waited at the station for Bellamy's tutor to arrive.

'I bet he's going to be awful,' said Terence.

'I expect he'll be jolly nice,' said the loyal and hopeful Bellamy.

As a matter of fact he was neither. He was just entirely non-descript, and made Esme's heart sink even further. He came, it seemed, from an improbable Oxford college which had recommended him on account of his excellent character. His name was Jeremy Clair, and he had spots, spectacles, and a 'belief' in Socialism. It was all rather depressing.

Conversation on the way back was desultory.

'It seems you're going to Scotland,' said Esme.

'That will be very nice,' said Jeremy Clair.

'I don't think it's a bit nice,' said Bellamy.

'Gosh, you're ungrateful,' said Terence.

Everyone shifted uneasily.

'Have you met Mrs Fairweather yet?' asked Esme.

'No, not yet,' said Jeremy Clair, 'I was interviewed by her lawyer.'

'Well, you've got a shock coming,' said Terence.

'I'm sure Mother will like you very much,' said the warm-hearted Bellamy.

There was another silence.

'Do you like shooting, Mr Clair?' Bellamy enquired kindly.

'Don't you think you ought to call me "sir",' said Jeremy Clair.

This went down very badly indeed. No tutor had ever been called 'sir', and it was unthinkable that the practice should start now.

'It's not usual in the family,' said Esme uneasily.

'Quite right, Esme,' said Terence embarrassingly.

Bellamy giggled.

'I will call you "sir" if you really like it,' he conceded.

'That's all right,' said Jeremy Clair stiffly.

A further pause.

'Was it you who was telling me how pompous Oxford men are?' said Terence innocently to Esme.

'No,' said Esme firmly, 'I like them very much.'

'How did it go?' went on Terence absently, ' "An Oxford man stands on his dignity like a tart who can't get" – '

'I never said anything of the kind,' said Esme, 'and in any case Mr Clair comes from Oxford.'

'Do you?' said Terence, 'but it wasn't me who made that bit up, it was Es—'

'Shut up,' said Esme fiercely. Mercifully, they had arrived.

If the day had started badly, it went on no better. Lunch was a nightmare.

'. . . The really irritating thing,' Esme was saying, 'is that Terence and I were just beginning to get very interested in sailing. We were getting along rather well.'

A gleam of interest came into Jeremy Clair's face.

'What sort of craft were you using?' he asked.

'Oddly enough,' said Esme guiltily, 'I never really asked the man what it was. It – it – just had a sail,' he concluded.

'He should have told you,' said Mr Valley, 'it's generally the first thing you're taught – to know and appreciate your tackle. What sort of crewmen did you and Terence make?'

'I was told I was jolly good,' said Terence. 'Esme was a bit slow at first, but he got into it quite w—'

'What stations did you take?' asked Mrs Valley.

'Well,' said Esme, 'Terence used to sit in the front, and I used to sit in the back, and—'

'Bow and stern,' said Jeremy Clair reprovingly. Esme began to hate Jeremy Clair.

'I mean, Terence used to sit in the stern, and I used to sit in the bow, and—'

'But you said,' Mr Valley remarked sternly, 'that Terence used to sit in the front, which is the bow and you—'

'That's what I meant,' said Esme wildly, 'and the instructor used to do things with the sail, and then we used to do them as well, and—'

'What did you used to do?' asked Mrs Valley.

'Well, we used to put it so that it caught the wind.' Desperation drove him to poetry. He remembered something he had once been told. 'Going along was like flying with the birds,' he said.

Glances were exchanged, but Bellamy, who had a fair idea of what was going on, managed to shift the subject.

'Has my gun been kept clean?' he asked.

'I must say I think Bellamy's very lucky,' said Mrs Chaser.

'It's very lucky for everyone,' said Mrs Valley who had been in Sandra's room half the morning harping on the subject, 'because now that there – er – won't be too many people here, Terence and Mr Sa Foy can stay as long as Sandra wants them to. No need for anyone to rush about.'

'Yes,' said Mrs Chaser, 'everything can be carefully and suitably arranged.'

'Yes,' agreed Sandra, 'there's a lot to be considered. Dr Trito thinks they ought to motor through France.'

'That would be great fun,' said Mrs Valley, 'provided the van's repaired in time. They tell me petrol's the most terrific price on the Continent now, but with economy in other directions – like cinemas – they should get along very well.'

'Terence and Mr Sa Foy would never be happy outside a cinema for long,' said Mrs Chaser, 'Mary says they went every night when they were last here.'

'There was a crop,' said Esme, 'of excellent English films, two of which Dr McTavish had recommended as "portraying the essence of English culture". They were very stimulating.'

'I'm sure you'll find the French ones equally stimulating,' said Mrs Valley, and the subject was allowed to lapse.

Everywhere you looked, thought Esme when they were having coffee, there was nothing but hostility and procrastination. That loathsome Chaser woman with her knitting, the Valleys petting the favourite dachshund and saying how well kept he was, Sandra running up and down after a lighter she'd lost, Bellamy pretending to look for it, and now, on top of it all, Jeremy Clair who liked sailing – and what was he doing? Taking a pill. For his digestion, Esme supposed. Well, he hoped it choked him. It could hardly do that. What else could he hope for? YES. WHAT ELSE?

That evening he said to Terence, 'What did you do with those pills you gave your mother? The ones that make people's water red?'

'She threw them away,' said Terence, 'but I've got one odd one in a drawer. What do you want it for?'

'Can you keep a secret?' asked Esme.

'Sure.'

'Well, I rather agree with you about pompous Oxonians – especially when they start showing off about their sailing.'

'I'll buy that one,' said Terence, 'top right-hand drawer, at the back.'

Once again it meant choosing one's moment with care. Once he was in the train to Scotland Jeremy Clair could fall down dead for all the good it would do anyone. The shock must not come too soon.

On Friday night, after the boys had gone to bed, Esme suggested a drink.

'There's some whisky on the sideboard,' he remarked.

'I don't usually drink it,' said Jeremy Clair.

'You want to have just a very little with a bottle of Coca-Cola – you'll sleep like a bomb,' said Esme.

'Well, I don't suppose it can do me any harm.'

'Not unless anyone puts something in it,' said Esme jovially. 'You go into the library and I'll bring them in.'

The next morning at breakfast Jeremy Clair looked worried.

'You know, it's very odd,' he said to Esme, 'I feel quite all right, but the most peculiar thing's happened.'

'What?' said Esme.

He whispered in Esme's ear.

'Oh,' said Esme, looking rather shocked, 'well hadn't you better see a doctor – your own doctor, in the circumstances?'

'It's not very convenient – isn't there a local man?'

'He's the biggest gossip in the county,' said Esme, 'he and Sandra spend hours at it.'

'But what do you suppose is the matter?'

'Well that rather depends,' said Esme with a meaning look, 'but when it occurred in India, people used to disappear to hospital for several weeks.'

'Oh,' said Jeremy Clair.

'Well, if you're going to London or to your own man at home, look in and have a word with Sandra. It may make a difference to her arrangements.'

'Fibula,' said Sandra over the telephone, 'the most bloody thing's just happened. That ridiculous Clair young man has come in here and told me he's got something wrong with him. He said he couldn't exactly explain what it was, but he'd have to see his doctor and might even have to go into hospital. He looked a bit worried, I must say. But you see what it means? Bellamy can't go off without him, and that means keeping him here with Terence, and you said that was the worst thing poss—'

'What are you going to do?' asked Trito.

'I don't know from Adam, darling, but you *must* come down and help me out. If thingamy goes into hospital it'll just muck up everything.'

'This is a little sudden, Sandra, and I have got a lot of patients . . .'

They both knew the formula.

'But never mind that, darling, you know it'll be made up. Now please come quickly – I'm very worried and you know that's bad for me.'

'All right,' said Dr Trito, 'I'll just have a word with my secretary.'

He rang off and walked into the next room.

'I'm off for the day,' he announced. 'Please make an addition to the Fairweather account – item £15 services, item £5 expenses, item £10 for appointments cancelled.'

'But you've only got one app—'

'Who told you to start thinking for yourself,' snarled Trito and vanished through the door.

Down at Badlock there was chaos.

'The trouble is,' said Esme to Sandra, 'it's too late now to engage another tutor. Everyone's gone abroad or something by now. You'll just have to wait till Clair's all right again.'

'Oh God,' said Sandra, 'that means I'll have to look after Bellamy myself. Oh God, oh God, oh God.'

'But I'm sure Dr Trito will think of something.'

'But I can't possibly take Bellamy up to those awful Lanchesters. They all just huddle there – all seven of them – all too drunk, too mad or too poor to leave the place.'

'I should wait till Dr Trito arrives.'

'And Bellamy's so stupid it's like living with a kangaroo – a nice kangaroo, of course, but it's torture.'

'Dr Trito will know what to do.'

That was what everybody said. They said it the whole morning, till it began to have an hypnotic effect on Sandra – Trito, Trito, Trito – and by the time he arrived he had assumed, for her at least, the proportions of a demigod.

'Fibula, darling,' she wailed, 'whatever am I going to do? Mr Sa Foy says we shall never get another tutor, I *can't* take Bellamy to Scotland, we shall just have to wait for that horrible Mr Clair, *please* say what I must do.'

'Poor Sandra,' said Mrs Valley, 'you really must try and – '

'We'll have a little drink and some lunch,' said Trito, 'and then discuss it all – quietly and alone,' he said, looking round at the regiment assembled.

By the time Jeremy Clair had sheepishly returned with the news that there was nothing wrong with him, everything had been arranged. Sandra, who was beyond the dictates of logic and was attending only to those of panic, had quietly accepted everything that Trito had to say. Yes, she must stay calmly at Badlock with Bellamy till they knew what was wrong with Mr Clair. If nothing was wrong, then Bellamy could go off to Scotland as planned and only a day or so late. Meanwhile they must assume the worst and take immediate action – Terence and Bellamy had been together quite long enough. There was now no question of the detailed arrangements necessary for a motoring tour, but the secretary must ring up at once and book two air passages to Paris for Esme and Terence and two railway seats from there to Biarritz. She must also arrange for rooms at some hotel – did Sandra know of one? – good, the Hôtel du Palais. She could make additional reservations, while she was about it, for Sandra and Trito to proceed there later – after they had settled the business of Bellamy, and Sandra had had a good rest. For he was afraid she was very run down after the strain she had been under – for that, if no other reason, she mustn't think of leaving Badlock for Scotland – and he advised her to stay in bed. He was going to clear the Valleys and Mrs Chaser back to London : they merely cluttered the place up and got right on her tired nerves. Here was something to make her sleep – but she had better give her instructions to the secretary first. After that, she need have no worries at all, he'd take care of everyone, everyone. . . .

Dr Trito had done a splendid job. The secretary was summoned and told to make the reservations, and then to pack. The Valleys weren't even summoned – they were just told to pack. Esme who with everything else had just received a registered envelope, presumably from Mr Chynnon, containing five pound notes, felt his soul lift within him. The blackest of looks could not come near him now; it was his justification, his triumph, almost his apotheosis.

'Gunwales to you,' he almost screamed aloud as the Valleys steamed out of the station.

# XIII

Even in her worst moments Sandra never forgot the need to economize: so that Esme and Terence, in order to get tourist rates, had to get on an aeroplane very early in the morning – Tuesday morning.

Not until the 'plane was off the ground did Esme feel entirely safe. At any minute, he felt, the figure of Mrs Chaser might be seen rushing across the airfield with the news that Sandra had changed her mind due to the discovery of some new and really appalling iniquity. But nothing happened. They seated themselves right at the front, where, Terence said, they would be served first with any refreshments that might be going; and very soon were circling securely over outer London.

Now that they were off, there was a great deal to be thought about. The complexities of the intrigue for tickets had been so great that Esme had almost begun to forget there would be anything to do when he arrived. It was rather as though one would alight at Biarritz station to find the municipal band drawn up and the mayor in front of them ready to hand Esme £1,000 in Bank of England notes with a deft word of congratulation. Now that they were actually going there, the whole affair began to assume very different proportions.

In the first place, there were all the old objections as to the oddity of Chynnon's conduct and the doubtful genuineness of his offer. True, the fact that he had begun to send his £5 instalments when they became due seemed to mitigate these a little. But did they? If you supposed he was up to something different, something for which the whole Acre business was merely a cover, then the continued receipt of payment was not necessarily reassuring – especially as the information he had so far received amounted to nothing whatever save assurances of effort.

And now Biarritz was more or less a reality, there was a whole swarm of new problems to be tackled : of these the focussing point was, of course, Uncle Bill Gomery. According to the 'Luritania Supplement' he was going to be staying, like themselves, at the Hôtel du Palais (presumably for the same reason – i.e. to be within easy reach of the Duke of Panton). Again, since he was Bellamy's godfather and an old friend of the family, there would be no difficulty whatever about getting in touch with him. But there-after was a complete blank. How did one start pumping him? One couldn't just march up and say, 'I understand you once received Mrs Fairweather's very intimate confidences on the subject of her second husband : I have been offered a high price for these, so I should be obliged to you for a statement.' What was Uncle Bill's line? If he depended solely for support on his poor old novels, he might be glad of a cut. But this somehow seemed unlikely. Was he then of an indiscreet disposition? Did he talk in his cups? And if so, how easily did you get him into his cups? Most Americans were apparently remarkably forthcoming when you first met them, and then, when you really wanted to know something, sealed up like clams. Well there was nothing to be done about this until he had met Uncle Bill. Perhaps – who knew? – his Achilles heel would be as prominent as his nose.

Then there was another thing that worried him. What was the quality of Uncle Bill's secret? Mr Chynnon wanted something he could use against a woman 'whose life has been erratic but not lubricious . . . something verifiable by myself'. Uncle Bill's secret might be as true as the day but so improbable that it just wouldn't have sales-value without some sort of proof. He might, in short, produce something that, while true, might just as well have been made up – something entirely useless to Mr Chynnon for the execution of 'his act of justice'. Esme, sitting where he was now, over a B.E.A. breakfast and thousands of miles from Palm Beach, could think of five hundred different tales to fit the facts of the Acre suicide. Uncle Bill's would presumably be a true one – if he got it – but would be just as useless as the rest, very likely, unless there were some proof. And even if you dosed Uncle Bill with enough champagne to make him spill the beans, it was hardly likely that he would possess, still less likely that he would produce, the relevant documents, which in any case had probably long since been destroyed. But once again it was no use worrying till he'd seen and heard for himself.

When they landed in Paris they were swept off in one of the airport buses (a marked contrast to the sedate B.E.A. affair that had brought them out of London) and deposited at Les Invalides. From now on no one took any interest in them at all. They were alone and anonymous. Esme began to have, as he always did on these occasions, a feeling of complete release and safety. No one was watching, no one gave a damn. You did exactly as you chose. Blessed anonymity! Who cared if the taxi-drivers cheated you? Or if your bills in England were stacked a yard high? Here you could do anything – you could even, when the time came, extract intimate secrets from Mr William Gomery, you could even, he told himself, sell them to Mr Chynnon at immense prices and no matter how improbable they were.

After lunch on the train he preserved, for a time, his feeling of uplift. But it was getting very hot and the countryside was very dull. They had been up early and he was near sleep. One figure, however, kept hovering before his eyes, smiling and elusive, Dr Fibula Trito. There had always been an enigmatic quality about the man, an atmosphere of interrogation lying just beneath the surface – beneath the surface, because somehow the questions were never put, the man had an hypnotic faculty about him which compelled one to accept him at face value and without enquiry. But even his face value was, to say the least of it, very shaky currency. Esme, released at last from the inhibitions caused by Trito's constant imminence and wrapped around by that state of drowsiness combined with clear thinking which often precedes sleep, began, for the first time, to formulate a few of the problems presented by the doctor's really rather extraordinary behaviour.

In the first place, almost the very moment he had first met Esme he had drawn him slap into the centre of a major conspiracy. He had just sat down over a bottle of claret and, without warning or invitation, held forth, pungently and at length, on ways and means of cheating their joint employer. Well, not cheating her perhaps, but at any rate extracting her juice by the pint. He had then defied all the known rules of professional etiquette by denigrating a colleague in the coarsest terms, and had gone on to make it abundantly plain that, if there was anything wrong with Terence, the good God could take care of that while they took care of themselves. All this he had made appear the most natural thing in the world. Now Esme was prepared for a money-grubbing fraud, he was prepared for a voracious shark, but now he came to think of it in something like objective terms, he ought really to have been very shocked indeed to find himself being openly treated with the most villainous complicity. Why didn't Trito keep his villainy to himself? Wasn't it rather a risk to reveal himself? And why had Esme of all people been selected for the revelation?

And that wasn't all. Trito had continued to give assistance on all occasions and in the most equivocal way : throughout a series of rows, eruptions and rumours he had persistently appeared with sly words of comfort and assurance of renewed efforts at deceit. Above all he had espoused the cause of their journey to Biarritz as though the journey had been a holy pilgrimage and he, Trito, the Pope. In the end it was Biarritz that the whole thing boiled down to. 'I'm rather taken by the idea of Biarritz,' he had said : and 'I'm afraid this may cause rather a delay over Biarritz' . . . 'don't worry, I'll do my best' . . . 'cheer up – she's bound to send you off when the mood takes her.' And then, at the climax, he had shown unyielding insistence that the time had come and Sandra must at once send them off to Biarritz. It was the most consistent, if not perhaps the most odd, trait in the whole of the man's behaviour. . . . 'Taken by the idea of Biarritz' . . . 'Delay over Biarritz.' . . . 'Something to look at in Biarritz.' . . . 'Biarritz' . . . 'Biarritz.' . . . He woke up with a start, to find Terence shaking him and saying something about 'Bordeaux' and 'changing'. The taste in his mouth was appalling, the confusion of luggage and patois-speaking porters was frantic. But throughout this discomfort his thoughts, which must have been busy in his sleep, were as plain and insistent as the day. The moment he was woken up, there it was, overwhelming him, ringing through his head, explaining everything. Trito was Chynnon's agent too. It was as simple as that.

If he were Chynnon, and wanted reliable and intimate information about Mrs Fairweather, to whom, were it possible, would he turn? (Mais Biarritz, où est le voiture pour Biarritz?) To the Valleys? Or Miss Chaser? Too stupid. To the servants? Too indiscreet. To the Tutor? Perhaps – but of necessity only for a short time. (Mais on *dit* qu'il faut changer : quel étage, je vous en prie, pour Biarritz?) But who was a permanent, intelligent, much trusted and, above all, privileged member of Sandra's entourage? (Merci, merci : they settled in with a sigh.) Now Dr Trito was her doctor and her psychologist, her son's doctor and psychologist, her friend of long standing, her very present hope in every species of trouble. Admittedly it would take subtlety and care to establish, without risk, that he was also sufficiently unscrupulous to undertake the employment Chynnon had in mind, but the task was not impossible.

Very well then, assume the task successfully completed, an agreement arrived at, what followed? Obviously that it was Trito who had gathered all the information, – and his position for the task was unrivalled – from the past history of Sandra's husbands to the present engagement of himself as tutor; and furthermore, that in all probability he, Trito, had been consulted by Chynnon about the advisability of employing Esme as an extra hand, had presumably (if reluctantly) consented, and had then proceeded to withhold vital information from Esme (witness the absence of Gomery from the list he had been given), information which in any case he was probably going to keep to himself, lest Chynnon should trace the secret by his own efforts and thus see no necessity to produce a reward. As for his complicity with Esme – well he might indulge it! It was hardly likely that Esme would start carrying tales of any sort, even if he believed himself unsuspected in his own particular line. Take it a little further: somehow or other Trito had also got on Gomery's trail, had taken good care, as he believed, to see that Esme didn't, and was not, unnaturally, extremely anxious to get to Biarritz on his own account. Terence at Biarritz was just where Trito wanted him – had he not announced his intention of following them with Sandra? Meanwhile the innocuous Esme, as Trito conceived it all, would be fiddling about in blissful ignorance of Uncle Bill's importance and to no good effect whatever, and would finally be sent home, forty odd pounds to the good, but otherwise no further on.

But this raised an objection. Why had he, Esme, been employed at all? Granted Chynnon still thought he had a real if slender chance of solving the mystery, wasn't it enough to have Trito working for him – especially if the addition of Esme gave Trito cause for annoyance? This it would almost certainly do, what with the possibility both of competition and interference. And if they so far distrusted him that they had employed him without telling him he had an ally, why hadn't they just observed him for a few weeks, instead of committing Mr Chynnon to expense and perhaps to risk at the moment of his commencing as tutor and on the strength of his not really very villainous past?

Still, if this new hypothesis created a minor difficulty, it solved many major ones. It solved the whole problem of Trito's behaviour: and it settled the question of the very arbitrary list Chynnon had given Esme. For he no longer had any worries on Chynnon's score: indeed it was Chynnon who was being taken for the ride by Trito. Yes, that was obviously it. In the same way as he himself, for various reasons, had told Chynnon nothing at all, Trito, likewise, was holding out on the old man – hoping no doubt to produce the information as a *fait accompli* and collect his prize on the spot. They neither of them, Esme or Trito, wanted Chynnon muddling round Uncle Bill and getting the story for himself.

But if from the point of view of logic this was all highly satisfactory, from other points of view it was quite the reverse. So far Esme had believed that, on the whole and despite the possibility of Chynnon's duplicity, he, Esme, was the only man living on the trail of the Acre secret. Even so things were quite hard enough. But under the newly developed Trito hypothesis, the doctor's hitherto unexplained zeal for the boys to visit Biarritz could now be interpreted in one light only. Trito also was on the track of Uncle Bill. True, he had given Esme, whom he did not know to be in the running, an odd seven days' start; but now, instead of assessing the position with care and getting slowly and tactfully to work, Esme would have to blast the secret straight out of Uncle Bill and have it safely in Chynnon's hands, all, if his success was to be assured, within a week. It was a discouraging prospect. He could only be thankful that his revelation, though late, was not too late. At least he knew how he stood. They were now about two hours off Biarritz: the two hours would expire – and then the race was on.

# XIV

As they arrived very late it was not until the next morning that they had a chance to examine their surroundings.

The Hôtel du Palais started life and ended it as a royal residence. It is now a morgue. But a particularly interesting morgue, because in it you are enabled to observe every stage of living death, from incipient atrophy of the mental organs up to total paralysis through inertia.

The earlier stages are the more interesting (wholesale collapse tends to obscure diagnosis) and are instanced, very largely, by the more recent Continental set, whose decay has been retarded for ten years by the intervention of the war. But perhaps laboratory is a better word than morgue. For if the specimens exhibited are gangrenous, no one could say they are obsolete. They have the recommendation of representing a life force. For let there be no mistake in this matter – the Continental set is no more on its way out than the internal combustion engine. If anything far less so, because the slackening of its social standards (which were admittedly never very high) has led to the recruitment of a magnificent selection of socialist politicians, Greek syndicateurs, and Near-Eastern catering magnates with a profitable sideline in drugs. Every breed is strengthened by new blood : the blood now flowing into the Continental set has the perennial robustness of corruption; and thus the diseased stem of the international pleasure-finance world is putting forth blooms more exotic and vicious than have ever before been observed.

These latter remarks may be taken (since both politics and finance are easily subsumed under crime), to refer to the criminal section of the *haute monde* of the pleasure grounds. This section has the advantage of being amusing, tolerant, and necessary. Drugs, drink, sex, socialist doctrine, and armaments are all required to keep the world revolving at its usual merry pace. Again, the members of this section only begin to decay above the neck when they finally decide on retirement. Far more objectionable, and totally without any function other than the admittedly vital one of being exploited by the criminals, is the second, and obverse, and more obviously moribund, section of this world, the people who tend to come to the Hôtel du Palais (the criminal's tendency is for the Miramar) and in whom the dominant feature is the hebetude which first prompted these observations. Their friends from the Miramar are, of course, often to be seen busy fleecing them in the entrance lounge of the Palais, but the residential support of the latter hotel springs largely from this second, duller, more odious, and morally more worthy class, namely the passive half of the European smart set. They are the hosts of the parasites (though they mingle, of course, on terms of social equality), and it is admittedly a purely personal taste that is expressed in the form of a preference for the slickness of the parasites as against the passive stupidity of the hosts. As has indeed been remarked it is the infiltration of a new and peculiarly venomous genus of parasite into the actual realms of social activity that has ensured the continual survival of the Continental set *in toto*. They suck in blood, the parasites, but their excrement is the very stuff of the ground on which they drop it.

Now it was the custom of His Grace the Duke of Panton to settle for a month or so every summer in the Hôtel du Palais, and there to gather round him possibly the most nauseating specimens that pertain either to the parasitical class or its obverse. His particular fondness was perhaps for the obverse; and during the month in which the Palais enjoyed his patronage, the full flower of the Church-bound Spanish nobility, the money-bound English nobility and the hide-bound French nobility were to be seen in Biarritz. This was good for trade and excellent for advertisement: so that after the Duke had continued in this habit through the early thirties the local syndicate undertook to pay his entire expenses (an offer they renewed after the war) conditional only on his repeating every year for the benefit of the local paper how preferable was Biarritz to Cannes, how infinite in diversion, and how incomparable in matters both of hygiene and natural beauty.

(It was His Grace who made the noted and poetical comparison of the surf-swept beach to sweating pelote players).

It was then the 'Duke's month' that provided the Palais with the bulk of its annual profits and the entire flavour of its atmosphere. It was slap in the middle of the 'Duke's month' that Terence and Esme arrived : so that they found the whole building, the whole staff, the whole cuisine, and the whole tone more pointedly itself than at any other time. The whole place, in short, was more efficiently geared than ever to fulfil the requirements of the pomp and circumstance that attend ineptitude. The *à la carte* menu was longer, the *virs du jour* were poorer, the waiters took more tips, the page-boys suffered more winks, the maids discovered more truths and the manager told more lies, than at any other period of the year.

And so it was that, on a fine Wednesday morning in the first week of August, they awoke to find themselves with rooms facing the old and voracious Atlantic in one direction and the almost equally old and voracious ocean of fashionable squalor and fanatic procrastination in the other.

The first thing Esme told Terence that morning was that they must get in touch with his Uncle Bill.

'Aw, hell,' said Terence, 'there's plenty of time for that. You seem to have Uncle Bill on the brain.'

'Your mother would be very angry if she knew we were under the same roof and hadn't done anything about it.'

'Since when are you worrying about her?'

This was a difficult one.

'Anyhow,' said Esme, 'he sounds very interesting. There are his novels, and – '

'Now for the last time I'm telling you : Uncle Bill would have gone under as a pulp writer. It's only his cash that keeps him going with more or less decent houses. His books would make a fish squirm.'

'Have you read any?'

'Sure I've read some. He sends them all to Mother – he even dedicated one to her. *The Cheese in the Trap* he called that one.'

'What was it about?'

'A small boy at school in the Middle West, who used to go to his fairy glade for the week-end. One Saturday he found a real, live fairy there – '

'I think I've got it,' said Esme hurriedly : 'how did it end?'

'Well, this Saturday in fairyland turned the boy right up. He ran loose around the woods and the rivers, and one day plunged right in a lake because it was so "pure and cool". He was looking for purity, see, after what happened in the glade. Well, he couldn't get himself out again, so he just drowned in the moonlight.'

'How sad,' said Esme.

'About as sad as a heap of dung,' said Terence : 'Uncle Bill's books make me retch.'

'But isn't he quite pleasant just to meet?'

'Fruity, that's what he is, as fruity as Grade I ketchup. He'll just drop off his tree one of these days and burst on the floor in a big red mess.'

'Fruitiness implies some sort of tang,' said Esme self-consciously.

'Uncle Bill's got as much tang as Dead Sea fruit,' said Terence.

'Well, we're going to ring him up and ask him to dinner anyhow,' announced Esme firmly : 'then, we'll do whatever you like for the rest of the day.'

'That's if you can get him,' replied Terence : 'he'll probably be busy gumming himself to the Duke of Panton's evening breeches.'

Esme attached himself to the telephone and asked to be put through to Monsieur Gomery. A girl's voice answered – a very young girl's voice – and said it would fetch its Uncle Bill at once.

'Hullo, there,' said a syrupy boom.

'Mr William Gomery?'

'That's right,' said Uncle Bill with satisfaction.

'Well, this is Terence Fox's tutor here. I understand you're a great friend of Mrs Fairweather's, and Terence and I hoped you'd come and have dinner with us tonight.'

'So Terence is right here in Biarritz?' said Uncle Bill. 'Sure I'd just love to see him again. Bellamy too?'

'No, Bellamy's gone to Scotland.'

'Swell, the kid always liked Scotland, I guess the tang the heather gets inside him. But you're asking me to dinner?'

'That's it,' said Esme.

'Well, I'd love to come, but you'll have to let me bring Maisie along. Maisie and I go everywhere together. The poor kid'd cry her pretty eyes out if I left her alone for the evening.'

137

'That's all right,' said Esme, 'Terence and I would love to meet Maisie. Eight o'clock in the bar for a drink. All right?'

'Great,' said Uncle Bill as though his mouth was full of paw-paw, 'that's great. So long.'

'Well?' said Terence.

'He's coming, and so's Maisie.'

'Who in hell's Maisie?'

'Well, if it was Maisie that answered the 'phone, she sounds about fifteen. It seems they go everywhere together and Maisie would cry her eyes out if she was left alone. She calls him Uncle Bill too.'

'Sounds like another of Uncle Bill's sham nieces,' said Terence cynically. 'Sure he hasn't any nephews stringing along?'

'He didn't say so.'

'Well, he will have when he's parked Maisie. It's six and half-a-dozen with Uncle Bill.'

'What do you suppose happens to Maisie?'

'No one quite knows,' said Terence. 'He says he likes young people around to remind him of his youth. I guess a lot of people say that. I reckon Maisie gets bathed and kissed and put to bed.'

'But how long's this been going on?'

'Since the war. It makes Mother mad. She says Uncle Bill's had a change of life.'

'Hm,' said Esme. 'Well, we'll get a good look this evening.'

And so they did. Uncle Bill, on his arrival at the bar, made an instant impression of immense size and a kind of squelchy boyish-ness. Maisie was rather pretty, loaded up with sex, and was pro-bably about nineteen: since, however, the way to Uncle Bill's heart was through an unceasing demonstration of adolescence, she was doing her best – and though highly artificial, it was a good best – to reproduce the pouts and whimsies, the dress and make-up, of a girl of sixteen. What gave her away was the omission of any sort of gawkishness or shyness. To say the least of it, she was adroit – so adroit that all the artlessness of all Mary Webb's hero-ines put together could not have disguised the fact. Uncle Bill, however, had evidently been too busy worrying about the per-manency of his wave to notice this.

'It was swell of you to ask l'il Maisie along,' he said in a voice like a bar of Ex-Lax, 'she just knows no one in these parts – do you, my little lonely one?'

'I know a few people thanks to dear Uncle Bill,' said Maisie. The cockney just came through the lisp.

'So when I told her about tonight,' went on Uncle Bill, 'she opened her big blue eyes at me and said, "Gee, Nuncle Bill" – just like that – "Gee, Nuncle Bill, it's so exciting, please buy me a new dress to meet them with." So we spent a great day in the shops, Maisie and I, and we've bought her some dandy outfits.'

Which would doubtless, thought Esme, come in handy when Maisie was, as Terence put it, parked.

Aloud he said, 'Now what will you all have to drink? Miss Maisie?'

'You must call me just Maisie,' she said with a simper, 'an' I'd like a nice citron drink with plenty of sugar.' Her eyes were hungry for a cocktail.

'Maisie don't drink much,' said Uncle Bill, 'not yet – but she's crazy about champagne, aren't you, honey?'

'Have some champagne now,' suggested Esme.

'No, not yet,' pouted Maisie, putting her head on one side like Shirley Temple, 'I have to be very careful still – don't I, Uncle Bill?'

'Of course, baby,' said Uncle Bill, 'at your age I should say you do.'

But if Maisie didn't drink much, Uncle Bill made up. It took 2,000 francs worth to get him in to dinner, and he showed no sign whatever of letting up. Esme ordered the most expensive meal he could pick out, and told the waiter to bring a bottle of champagne and keep three more on ice. If this was what they were in for, he was as game as Uncle Bill. And how Trito would approve when he heard! The champagne alone was going to set Sandra back for a clear 12,000 francs.

They made short work of the first bottle. Uncle Bill was undeniably in good form. His wave was coming down over his forehead more boyishly than ever.

'See that table over there?' he said, 'that's the Dook's table. I reckon the band are starting, and that means the Dook will be here any minute.'

Esme noticed that the drunker Uncle Bill became, the more

champagne went quietly down Maisie's pretty throat and the less she troubled with the Peggy Ann Garner act.

'There's the Duke now,' she said. He had just come in with the Duchess and a handful of the nastiest people in Europe. The Duchess (an American of low extraction) gave a great wave at Uncle Bill, the Duke smirked, and the nastiest people in Europe sneered. The band struck up triumphantly. Uncle Bill got up to bow, managed it, but sat down again on the floor. Esme helped him to his seat.

'That's all right,' said Uncle Bill, 'that's just l'il Maisie with her cute little tricks, moving my chair – wasn't it, honeybee?' he said with a leer, and took a great clutch at her thigh.

'You know I'd never play a mean joke like that on Nuncle Bill,' said Maisie, in a subtle and, Esme thought, purposeful, parody of her own manner, 'you just eat your lovely fritters and have some more champagne.'

What with the drink and the band and the heat, excitement was mounting all round. The waiter brought a third bottle, and Esme warned him to keep at least two more handy. The band, as a matter of fact, was really a pretty sickly affair, but just then it went on to play a romantic number from *South Pacific*, which, as Uncle Bill explained, just caught him in the throat. Great tears began to ooze over his flabby cheeks, and he looked at Maisie as though he wanted to button her into his waistcoat. Maisie was getting a sickener of Uncle Bill that evening, but managed a girl-wife smile.

Terence, meanwhile, had been fairly moderate, but wasn't used to champagne by the quart. He was getting very red and very talkative, and giving Maisie a series of looks, totally without sentiment, which threatened to clap horns on Uncle Bill before the next time he attended to his wave. For Maisie was anything but unresponsive; a mouth of soapsuds both in the bath and out of it had made a straight look doubly welcome; and Esme, whose legs were rather long, found himself mixed up, uninvited, in a little game under the table.

They began to get very noisy.

'This is a swell party I'll say,' roared Uncle Bill as the next bottle appeared, 'what d'ye say, little girl, a swell party?'

'Sure is,' said Maisie, warding off a grapple. 'What d'ye say, Terry, a toast all round?'

'A tes beaux yeux,' said Terence, with undeniable presence of mind.

'Yeah,' said Uncle Bill, 'to the prettiest little eyes, in the prettiest little head, on the prettiest little body, over the prettiest little legs in France.'

His free hand disappeared to give point to the observation.

'And another toast,' said Esme, 'to the great success of *Ten Dahlias in a Window Box*.'

This was a terrific hit.

'Gee but that's swell of you,' said Uncle Bill, 'that's mighty nice,' he said, flinging his glass over his shoulder to alight with a crash on an occupied table.

'Say, where did that pitch up?' he asked after the tinkle had penetrated his fuddled wits. 'I must say sorry.' He heaved himself up and waddled to the wrong table.

'You folks must pardon me,' he said, 'it's th' excitement of having the young folks around.' He made his point with a burp. They had finished eating, but another bottle had just arrived, and he swam back to his place. You could almost see the steam rise from him. Uncle Bill was stinking.

And the noise from the Duke's table was piercing.

'Aw, Bessy,' screamed a woman at the Duchess, 'who's that cute little boy over there, I could just crunch him up.'

'I don't know,' yelled the Duchess, 'but we'll get Bill to watch the fireworks with us later, and we'll all get cosy.'

'And there's a young man with a dandy forelock that makes my mouth water.'

'You just hold on till after the dessert,' screeched the Duchess. The band, who played more or less directly at the Duke's table, struck up with 'Under my Skin'.

'I've just gotchyou under my skin,' sang Uncle Bill, pouring his brandy down and choking till he went purple. 'Great stuff this, it just makes me wanna put l'il Maisie's head in my mouth and suck it like a sweetie.' Even he noticed the simile was somehow inappropriate.

'Waal, jush shuck it,' he said.

Later on they joined up with the Duke's party and went on to the terrace to watch the fireworks. These consisted in a display of the most magnificent rockets, fired singly and in shoals for an unbroken half-hour. Some of the effects were beautiful, others vulgar, and all striking.

But no one paid much attention to the fireworks. They happened every Gala night, and any night which wasn't a Festival night was a Gala night. A whole lot more champagne was ordered by Esme and the Duke (the evening was letting Sandra in for about 30,000 francs), everyone got into a confused and friendly huddle, and no one made the slightest attempt to conceal what they were doing, even when the largest rocket burst right over their heads like an indication of heavenly wrath.

Uncle Bill still had his head above water, and was sitting on one side and slightly in front of Maisie. On her other side and slightly behind her (he was learning fast) was Terence. Uncle Bill, then, was unable to see what Maisie was doing, but Esme could see only too well. He pointed it out to the Duchess's voracious guest, who took the hint : Terence was not for her but it was plain that Esme was. And as she told everyone afterwards, she might have happened worse. Esme was glad Terence was too well occupied to want any more champagne, because it would not have done him any good.

Shortly afterwards Uncle Bill, who was getting off his seat to reach for the bottle, fell flat and stayed put. No one took any notice for some time, till Maisie, who seemed to have dealt with this situation before, called up a pair of waiters.

'O.K., boys,' she said, 'pick up this lump of dirt and cart it off to bed. And keep your hands out of his pockets. That's my perk,' she told everyone without a blush.

'And now, darling,' she said with a lunge at Terence, 'we can settle in for a lovely evening. Rip van Winkle'll wake up in the morning and see the same world as ever.'

Terence found the new Maisie very exhilarating.

'How often does he fade out like this?' Esme called across.

'Four nights in seven since I've known him,' answered Maisie, 'it gives a girl a chance to lead her life. "L'il lonely one." I'm as lonely as the horns on his head.'

Esme looked up at the final cluster of rockets as they hovered to burst. It seemed to him that Uncle Bill must have had a very drastic change of life since he first received Sandra's confidences. A little liquor should do quite a bit with him. Item, he was a sot, item, he was an uxorious old billycock. If only he could make

Uncle Bill see what was up, he might trade an offer of assistance. Anyhow it was something to go on.

He steered his partner deftly off along the terrace.

'O.K.,' he said to Terence, 'you're on your own. But clear the decks before your uncle wants those dear l'il busy hands to mix his Alka-Seltzer.'

# XV

The next morning when he awoke Esme was not feeling quite at his best. But a little reflexion told him he had every reason for satisfaction. It was to be presumed that Terence had learned a few useful lessons on the previous night, and, which was more important, he had given Esme the lead for a possibly valuable line of action. Esme gave him till half past ten, and then went along to see him.

Terence was pale but pleased with himself.

'Well?' said Esme.

'It's even more fun than I thought,' said Terence.

This was excellent. None of Uncle Bill's nonsense about pure, cool lakes. Even temporary remorse on Terence's part would have been a harmful obstacle to what Esme had in mind.

'All well-brought-up boys have feelings of guilt and disgust,' said Esme heavily.

'They can keep their upbringing and their feelings.'

'Your problem,' said Esme, 'is to keep your girlfriend. I hope you'll take my advice.'

'Happen I shall.'

'Well then: the first thing you've got to do is to show a continued interest, looks and a bit of tickle. Got that?'

'Yes.'

'Then a certain amount of consideration is always a good thing. So here's 3,000 francs to be considerate with.' He tossed the notes over.

'Now then,' Esme continued, 'from principle to practice. Everyone in Biarritz spends the morning bathing. For this purpose there's a selection of three smart beaches. Do you know which one Maisie goes to?'

'She said the Chambre d'Amour.'

'A pretty name and the smartest beach of the lot. They tell me there's a sea-water swimming-pool there. Which is her – beach or swimming-pool?'

'Uncle Bill's got a chalet inside the swimming-pool compound. They have an awning in front with table and chairs, and there's a bar there too. So I guess that's where they'll be.

'Good enough,' said Esme. 'Uncle Bill's chalet will be a great convenience, I've no doubt his awning's a heavenly colour, and he owes us a few drinks after last night at the Chambre d'Amour bar. I shall take a book, you must go full of interest and consideration. Right?'

'Right,' said Terence.

'Then there's equipment. From a natural point of view you pass well enough, but in Biarritz a little artificiality is always a good thing. I should think a pair of dark glasses would help with the patches under your eyes and a pair of new bathing-trunks can do no harm. Money you've got – I have it – a present, you must give her a present at all costs. So we'll go to Cartier, you and I, and invest some of your mother's money in a simple but valuable object which Maisie's sharp eyes will know how to appreciate. But have the tact to give it her when Uncle Bill's not about. Right?'

'Right,' said Terence.

'Lastly,' said Esme, 'something to give you a bit of colour. So I'll thank you to get up while I summon two restoring drinks. Did you eat your breakfast?'

'Most of it.'

'Then you'd better have a sandwich as well. You may not know it, but you got rid of a lot of vitamins last night.'

'I don't doubt it,' said Terence happily.


When they arrived at Uncle Bill's chalet by the Chambre d'Amour swimming-pool, they were welcomed by looks as healthy as they were hearty. Uncle Bill looked positively radiant.

'It was a great party,' he said. 'Gee, but I'm sorry to have gone dead on you – I do that sometimes. My analyst says my reflexes are apt to give out if I get a bit excited.'

'That's all right,' they said.

'Now what about a drink?' said Uncle Bill (who to do him justice was the most generous of men). 'A little welcome to Chambre d'Amour for our friends Terence and Esme.'

'I'll just have a nice citron with some sugar,' said Maisie, who was definitely on duty again.

'What about you boys?' said Uncle Bill: 'I'll tell you what. We'll have a nice bottle of hock. It's the A1 morning drink.' Uncle Bill had his moments of appositeness it appeared. The hock came, and they settled peacefully down to lie still and say nothing. That was one of the charms of Biarritz. No one thought it odd if you spent the entire day out of the sun and on your back. After a bit Terence and Maisie went off to bathe.

'They make a swell pair,' said Uncle Bill, 'pretty little things. Innocence. That's what I like about kids. Innocence.'

'I gather that's the theme of one of your best-known books,' said Esme – '*The Cheese in the Trap.*'

'Yes,' said Uncle Bill wistfully, 'there's all of me in that book. L'il Ebenezer Coote who believed in fairies, and one day he comes up against the dirt of the world. It just finished Ebenezer, like it finished me. And ever since we've both of us been looking for something pure and cool to drown ourselves in, like I drown myself in Maisie.' He emptied his glass with a suck.

'Yes,' he said, refilling, 'innocence. And what a host of disillusions! Mr Sa Foy, Esme, what a host of disillusions! I'll tell you what I'm going to do, sir. Maisie an' I have been together a month now, an' I'm going in to San Sebastian 'cross the border to get her a big surprise this afternoon. It's an anniversary! So I'm going in to San Sebastian an' I'm going to get her a shawl we saw the other day. She said, "Nuncle Bill, I'm crazy about that shawl." And I said, "You shall have it, little potato, one day you shall have it." So this afternoon I'll go and get that shawl and bring it back as a big surprise. Then I'm going to order a swell dinner in my room with all the things she likes, and before we sit down I'll give her the shawl, and we'll have our anniversary feast.'

'You'll leave her alone for the afternoon?'

'Aw, she'll be a bit lonely maybe, but it's not for long. I've got to go alone to get the surprise.'

'You can leave her alone with confidence?'

'Sure. I don't ordinarily leave her, but l'il Maisie'd do nothing to get her Uncle Bill sore.'

'You know best, I suppose,' said Esme.

'Say, what's eating you, Esme? You don't have to be so sour.'

'It's never occurred to you that Biarritz might hold – temptations – for a young and attractive girl?'

'But Maisie's just a kid,' said Uncle Bill.

'So's Terence. He has ideas just the same.'

'Aw they're just a couple of sweet kids,' said Uncle Bill.

At that moment they came round the bath. Maisie stooped to examine her foot, and Terence made a neat pass from behind. Now surely, thought Esme, just what he'd been hoping for.

'Get a look at that,' said Uncle Bill, 'don't it make you feel good seeing those kids playing together – like two little pixies,' said the great booby, almost with a sob: 'I hope Maisie an' Terry'll see a lot of each other from now on.'

Of course it had been too much to suppose that Uncle Bill would fly into immediate tantrums of jealousy. What Esme had hoped was that he might perhaps be able to plant the seed. It now looked, however, as though Uncle Bill was really too crude a person to be dealt with by innuendo at all. There were such people, Esme knew, and they were incapable of seeing anything they didn't want to. On the whole he wasn't sorry Uncle Bill happened to be one. His progress by innuendo would have been a very slow and painstaking business however fertile the soil: as it was, there was nothing for it but to employ explosive tactics: and these might just as well be employed immediately, once granted the necessity for them was plain. It was hit or miss, of course; but he was now to be spared an agony of waiting.

And indeed there was a lot to be said in favour of that particular evening for what he had in mind. Uncle Bill was going sentimentally off into Spain to pick up Maisie's surprise: he would return prepared for an endearing little dinner *à deux*; and the contrast of what he had expected with what he was going to find should have a swift and laxative effect.

At lunch Esme said to Terence:

'There's a thing called the *Grand Guignol* showing at the theatre in the little Casino. It's just your thing I should imagine – lewdness alternating with beastliness.'

'It sounds good enough.'

'Now I'm going to get you a couple of tickets for this evening. But you're not to mention it to Maisie till I give the word.'

'Maisie says they're having a special dinner tonight to celebrate their first month's anniversary.'

'That's just the point. But I'll square it all for you provided you get Maisie out of the hotel this afternoon. Uncle Bill's going in to Spain at about three o'clock. After that get her out – take her to Bayonne or somewhere and spend some money on her – and bring her back in time to change and have an early dinner. The show starts at eight. But don't say anything about it till you get her back and see me.'

Now in point of fact San Sebastian, where Uncle Bill was going, wasn't very far, certainly not more than thirty miles. But the roads were narrow and dangerous, and so the journey might take as much as an hour and a half either way. Then it would take Uncle Bill some time to make his purchase; and there were formalities (passport, currency, customs) to be gone through at the border, both ways. Even so it was hardly likely that Uncle Bill would be home much later than seven. Mercifully, however, there was something wrong with his own car, and he was hiring one of the hotel fleet. It was not difficult to find the driver allotted to Uncle Bill : a thousand francs down, and the promise of a further thousand when Uncle Bill was safely delivered not earlier than eight-fifteen nor later than nine made the man quite cheerful at the thought of spending an hour or so lying under his engine pretending to look at the works. Somewhere isolated must be chosen, Esme emphasized – there would be no bonus if Monsieur Gomery started plaguing them all with telephone calls.

So far so good. Uncle Bill went happily off at three. Shortly afterwards Maisie and Terence got into another hotel car and vanished towards Bayonne. Esme retired for a siesta. There was now nothing to be done till Terence brought Maisie back.

This happened just after six. Esme was waiting for them in the hall.

'Uncle Bill's just rung up,' he told them, 'they've had a smash – nothing serious luckily, but the car's done in and Uncle Bill's a bit shaken, he says. They're giving him a few stitches and something to make him sleep, and he wants you, Maisie, to ring up tomorrow morning when he's himself again. He'll come back then.'

'He certainly does the right thing every now and again,' said Maisie, 'but I hope he doesn't breathe his last before he gets my "surprise" back. Now what do you say we do this evening, Terry?'

Esme nodded at Terence.

'Well, let's change and get some dinner,' said Terence, 'and then we might look in at the *Grand Guignol* for a start. O.K.?'

'O.K.,' said Maisie, 'half an hour and I'll see you in the bar. I'm going to miss Uncle Bill something fierce,' she said and flew towards the lift.

'Nice work,' said Esme, when Terence was changing. 'Now listen to me. Have you given her that bracelet yet?'

'No, I thought this even—'

'Right,' said Esme. 'Now I'm going to leave you to have dinner with her alone. Give her something to drink and then take her along to the theatre. Keep her going in the intervals, and then, when you come out, suggest a breath of fresh air and take her down to the beach just in front of the little Casino. It's supposed,' he said, 'to be a lucky spot for lovers. Tell her that, give her the bracelet, and then kiss her – don't just pick, go into a real clinch and use the two hands heaven gave you for the purpose. Then take her off to a café with an orchestra. Whatever you do, don't bring her home till late, really late. If you try and get home early, she'll think you just want her and not her company. And that makes women savage – even women like Maisie, who've no reason to expect anything else.' That was a bit sour, he knew, but, whatever happened, he mustn't suddenly find himself organizing a *grande passion*.

'Now have you got all that? Beach – present – grapple – café?'

'Yes,' said the grateful Terence. To do Esme justice his previous recommendations had resulted in the most satisfactory afternoon.

'Good,' said Esme; 'Well here are the tickets and I'll see you tomorrow. There's some more cash for you on the table. And don't forget – no hurrying home.'

At eight o'clock Esme settled down in the entrance hall to wait for Uncle Bill. He could only pray that Terence did what he was told and that Uncle Bill swallowed the hook. There was going to be a row in any case and he only hoped he was going to get his money's worth – literally as well as figuratively, for it had all been very expensive. In the circumstances it probably wouldn't – indeed it mustn't – get back to Sandra. On the whole, he thought, Uncle Bill was not likely to send in complaints if it meant explaining about Maisie.

At half past eight, a rather bedraggled Uncle Bill appeared in the doorway.

'Engine trouble,' he said disagreeably when he saw Esme.

'Come and have a drink,' suggested Esme.

'O.K., but where's my little girl?'

'I don't know,' said Esme awkwardly, 'at least I do in a way. She's with Terence.'

'But that's O.K.,' said Uncle Bill, 'they're around somewhere, those kids. We'll have that drink and then go and find them.'

He led Esme off to the bar. They had one drink and then another. The more the better, thought Esme, within limits. He ordered a third lot.

'Get the shawl?' he asked.

'Yeah. My little girl's going to fall over herself when she sees it. Where did you say they were?'

'I'm not quite sure.'

'Well, we'll go and find them in a minute.'

'That may not be too easy.'

'I'll send a page-boy round,' said the obtuse Uncle Bill.

'I mean, they're not in the hotel.'

'They'll be back. Maisie wouldn't keep her Uncle Bill waiting on a night like this.'

'Look,' said Esme, 'it's not easy for me to say this; but I went to my room just before you got back, and there was a note from Terence saying he'd gone out with Maisie. He said I wasn't to expect him back till very late.'

Uncle Bill looked at though he had been hit on the head with a steam shovel.

'I don't expect Terence knew about your dinner,' explained Esme.

Uncle Bill gulped.

'But l'il Maisie, she knew – '

'I know,' said Esme, 'and I'm sorry it's me that has to tell you this.'

'But what am I gonna do, Mr Sa Foy? I just can't believe that l'il Maisie'd—'

'I did try to warn you,' said Esme: 'these children get ideas in their heads. Terence is an – '

'Aw, Jese,' said Uncle Bill. 'Aw, Jese. And me just waiting to – '

'Now look,' said Esme, 'just stop worrying. They won't have gone far and they don't mean any harm. It's just thoughtlessness, childish thoughtlessness. You and I will go and have our dinner, and then we'll go out and look for them.'

'But we'd better start looking right away.'

'You're tired and hungry. Maisie'd never forgive herself if she thought her carelessness had made you too ill to eat. They won't be far.'

Esme cashed in on Maisie's anniversary dinner which had certainly been done in style. It was a pity he had to keep worrying about the time; but the *Grand Guignol* would be over by ten-thirty, Uncle Bill was really getting plastered, and he'd have to be steered off along the front, with a detour or two for effect, in good time to see everything intended for him. It had been nine-fifteen before they started eating.

'Whose idea d'ye suppose it was, to go off like this?' asked Uncle Bill.

'I couldn't say. Both of them, I suppose.'

'It's the first time that Maisie's ever run out on me. Our anniversary night, an' it's the first time.'

'I know,' said the sympathetic Esme. He hoped Uncle Bill wasn't going to pass out on him.

'But we'll waste no time, Mr Sa Foy. We'll eat our dinner and waste no time. Aw, Jese!'

Perhaps it was as well they would have to hurry dinner. It was not going to be a cheerful meal.

'O.K.,' said Esme after Uncle Bill had had three brandies to stiffen himself, 'we'll start down by the little Casino.'

'Why there?'

'It's on a piece of the front people are very apt to wander to in the evenings. There's a café facing over the sea with a band – and there are some side-streets before we get there with some places they might have gone to.'

'What sort of places?' asked the petulant Uncle Bill.

'Just restaurants.'

'Then let's get started. If I don't get my eyes on l'il Maisie inside of an hour, I'm going to call out the gendarmerie, that's what I'm gonna to do, I'm gonna c—'

'Now don't get hasty,' said Esme, 'that wouldn't do any good at all. You'd scare the life out of them.'

'Right now I'm having the life scared out of me.'

'Then finish your drink, and let's be off.'

The doorman gave the exaggerated salute he reserved for drunks. (Sometimes they thought he must have done something for them, and tipped him on the spot.) Esme piloted Uncle Bill unsteadily towards the hotel gate, up the rue Edouard VII, and then down some steps into a network of side-streets.

'Take it easy,' said Uncle Bill, 'we got to get a look in some of these places.'

It was hard work getting him to the front in time without moving faster than appeared consonant with their search. Sometimes he wanted to take looks inside places, and once they got downstairs to find themselves in a night-club called La Cave. A girl and a repellent negro were jiving on the floor.

'They won't be here,' said Esme.

'Never know . . . Say, has anyone seen two kids, a boy an' a girl,' roared Uncle Bill, lurching forward on to the dance floor. The negro's back-kick caught his shin, and he fell back with a crash on to a table.

'You'd better come out before we get a biff,' said Esme.

'Not till I've taught that bloody nigger better manners, I'll get the bast—'

'Shut up,' said Esme fiercely, 'they've got racial tolerance round these parts. They have to have,' he said, looking round at the appalling crew of mongrels who formed the clientele of La Cave. 'Come on, will you, you're making us l— you're delaying our search.'

His damaged shin had rather dampened Uncle Bill's curiosity. By the time they reached the café on the front – it was directly between the Casino and the beach – it was just after ten-thirty. Red lights above them advertised roulette and baccarat, the moon shone brightly on to the sea, and the orchestra struck up with a tango. The place was getting very full, Esme noticed. That might mean the *Grand Guignol* was over. Esme looked along the beach. The only cover was a pile of surf-boards, about fifty yards off the concrete front and a hundred yards to their left. He hurried Uncle Bill along till they were well past the surf-boards, found a vacant seat, and told him they'd earned five minutes' rest. Two minutes later – heaven be thanked – Terence and Maisie came down some steps from the Casino and then went down a few more from the front to the beach.

'It's quite all right,' he whispered to Uncle Bill, 'keep quiet and look at that.' Terence and Maisie were sitting on the surf-boards holding hands.

'Doesn't it make you feel good?' he asked Uncle Bill.

Just then Terence put his hand in his pocket, paused a moment, then slipped something on to Maisie's arm.

'He's giving her a present,' said Esme in the voice he'd been taught to use for his prayers.

'Aw, gee,' said Uncle Bill, the tears welling to his besotted eyes.

When the bracelet was on, Terence paused again for a moment. Then he made a fierce grab at Maisie, remembering every word Esme had spoken, pressed her to him till he seemed to crush her, and finally put his lips to her throat. Maisie just wilted with pleasure, and passed her fingers over his thighs like a cat scratching a rug. It was clear that Terence had talent.

Meanwhile, Uncle Bill had emitted a gasp of dismay and started to rise. Esme pulled him down and clapped a hand over his mouth.

'Keep quiet, will you?' he hissed. 'Do you want them to know they're being watched?'

Evidently that was just what Uncle Bill did want, for he struggled for some time; he was not very difficult to control, however, what with age and drink.

'Cool off,' said Esme. This was a little harsh on Uncle Bill, for the scene before their eyes was becoming almost primitive. After a minute or two more, however, Terence rose, put his arm round Maisie's waist and escorted her back up the steps. Esme released Uncle Bill.

'Where are they going?' spluttered the disillusioned sugar-daddy. As luck would have it the way up the steps was a possible start back to the hotel.

'Where do you suppose, after *that*?' said Esme.

'We must get back to the hotel,' said Uncle Bill, trembling all over, 'something terrible may happen.'

'Keep calm,' said Esme, 'they'll be having a bottle of champagne before anything starts.'

'We must get back at once.'

'All right. But don't work yourself into a stroke.'

'But gee, Esme,' said Uncle Bill, 'how could they do that – who told them how to do that? Those kids – aw gee.'

'It doesn't take lessons,' said Esme, 'and I warned you. Now slacken your pace or you'll fetch up in a mortuary.'

It was about five minutes' walk back to the hotel. The doorman gave an even more elaborate salute. Uncle Bill turned towards him and started to open his mouth.

'Belay that,' rapped Esme quickly, 'do you want the whole staff talking?'

'We must get to Terry's room – quickly,' said Uncle Bill.

'Nothing of the sort. We'll go to yours and talk things over. I've told you nothing'll start for a bit. You can't just burst in on him.'

Before Uncle Bill could object they were in the lift and the button had been firmly pressed. Esme swept him out and into his own room on the third floor. Then he shoved Uncle Bill on to the settee and locked the door behind him.

'Now we can talk in peace,' he said.

'What's there to talk about?' asked Uncle Bill.

'A whole lot,' said Esme; 'do you want to get down there before Terence and Maisie make a fool out of you?'

'Yeah, I do that, and what's more I'm goin' now, Mr Sa Foy, and nothin's gonna stop me.'

'You'll have to get the key first.'

'But you wouldn't ho—'

'That's all you know.'

'Say, what you after?' asked Uncle Bill, almost in tears again. 'I thought you were my friend, Mr Sa Foy, I thought – '

'So I am. But acts of friendship are reciprocal. Before we go there's something I want to ask you.'

'But that can keep,' howled Uncle Bill. 'I'll tell you what I know about anything I know about, but for heaven's sake let's – '

'We'll not move,' said Esme, 'until you tell me what I'm after. Do you know the number of Terence's room?'

'No, but – '

'Nor will you. I shan't tell you, and the man at the desk has 2,000 francs and orders to keep his mouth shut. If you want to blunder all over the hotel . . . But in any case you won't find it easy in your condition to get out of the room with me to stop you. Have you got that, Mr Gomery?'

Uncle Bill was now blubbering like a great whale.

'Anything, Mr Sa Foy,' he moaned, 'but be quick, will you? My l'il girl and – '

'Very well. Now I want you to tell me, Mr Gomery, everything you know about the circumstances attendant on the suicide of Mr Earl Marshal Acre.'

Uncle Bill's mouth fell open like a sick baboon's.

'What do you know about Earl Marshal Acre?' he gulped.

'Very little; but I have reason to believe – in fact, Mr Gomery, I *know* – that you have more information on the subject than any-one else living – with one obvious exception. Now then, will you tell your story?'

'But that was a confidence,' stuttered Uncle Bill, too drunk to realize he was giving himself away, 'that was an intimate secret between friends, Mr Sa Foy, you wouldn't ask me to tell you that.'

'I would,' said Esme, 'and I do. Time's getting short, Mr Gomery; what do you say?'

'What do I say?' He was now writhing with anguish on the settee. 'What do I say, Mr Sa Foy?'

'You heard me,' yelled Esme, 'get a hold of yourself.'

'I say "no", Mr Sa Foy,' said Uncle Bill, suddenly stung into showing a little moral courage : 'I say "no, sir" to your black-mailing, rascally face.'

'You do, do you?' said Esme savagely; 'well then, you fat, drunken ape – GET A LOOK AT THIS.'

'This' was his last card. It was the picture Terence had drawn at Aldeburgh.

Uncle Bill gaped. 'D ' ye mean to tell me – ?' he gasped.

'Yes I do. And I'll tell you something more. Where do you think they've been tonight? To the *Grand Guignol*, you blubbering booby, and Terence has come back with his head one mass of ideas. Can you take that in? Are you sober enough to see what it means?'

Uncle Bill was struggling for air and waving his hands about like an hysterical octopus.

'Then any minute now he may – ?'

'He very well may, Mr Gomery. Now give, will you, GIVE.'

Uncle Bill Gomery gave in – and gave.

It had all been very tiresome. It was an open question, very open, whether it had been at all worth it. It was a relief to find that Terence had followed his instructions to the last, and that no one was in his room. Even so, Uncle Bill and Maisie vanished early the next morning. Sandra might think Biarritz perfect for children, but Uncle Bill was taking his little chicken on to Cannes.

# XVI

So there it was. The Acre secret on a plate. It was a tale that would certainly put the cat among the pigeons: but there was no corroborative evidence of any kind whatever. And as bad luck would have it, it was essentially a tale that required support – probable enough in its way, which was always something, but it required support. He had anticipated this, of course, but it was discouraging to find his fears confirmed. But at the same time, was it ever likely to have been otherwise?

At lunch-time the next day Esme was still wondering what to do. Uncle Bill had gone, so that Trito hadn't a hope when he arrived, but then what sort of hope had he himself? The cash value of the story he could tell Mr Chynnon was probably about ten pounds over and above his salary due – ten pounds for a clever effort and a piece of information that might conceivably become useful if – and only if – a million to one chance came up and brought further evidence out of the blue. Now he had long ago jettisoned any chance of being able to save sixty pounds for the Bursar of his college by ordinary methods. His own tastes would probably have seen to that in any case, while the recent expenditure on Uncle Bill and Terence, much of which he would be compelled, he saw, to foot out of his own pocket, would now finally settle the question. He had grim visions of returning empty in October. . . . 'We've really given you every chance' . . . 'Liverpool University' . . . No, that was too much. . . . 'Send you out of those comfortable rooms of yours' . . . 'Live in the Milton Road – you'll have to buy a bicycle and cycle in to lectures' . . . Well, he wouldn't go to any lectures, damned if he would. . . . 'No more parties, of course, no one will want to go out all that way' . . . 'And I don't suppose there's a key to your door, so you won't be able to – '

This must stop. It might very well happen, but there was no point in getting morbid about it before it did. Still, what the devil was he going to do with his story? Tell it to Trito? Perhaps *he*'d push it with Chynnon. Perhaps he'd push a matchbox down St James's Street with his nose. Would it be any good to reveal the whole conspiracy to Sandra? And have any reward he might expect for that office cancelled out – and more – by the inevitable revelation of the part he himself had played. It was enough to madden a nun : here he was, having staked his chance of paying the Bursar – a definite chance with Chynnon's extra salary – against a remote offer of £1,000 : here he was, having fought almost incredible difficulties, first to get to Biarritz, then to pump Uncle Bill; and finally, here he was, having against all the odds earned his £1,000 – and with a rat's chance of getting the cash. It was really too unkind.

Consider the story again. Uncle Bill had been at school and college with Marshal Acre. Then, as later, Acre had been a joke. The biggest joke of all had been Acre's marriage. Why had it been a joke? Well, they all knew the answer to that one. A romantic passion was one thing, its implementation was another. But surely Sandra – Sandra, as usual, hadn't even thought about it – until they were married. Then she thought a good deal. For once in her life propriety had fought a losing battle. She had been disappointed, she had been cheated (always a strong point with her), in short she was furious. Ostensibly she had only been looking for a sort of chivalrous-squire-cum-general-bottlewasher (which she had certainly got) but when it came to the point . . . She reacted hard. One afternoon a sudden spell of sickness had stopped Acre's golf, he came back early, and found something that cured his chill right away. He was silent, hurt, he went out, he wrote a note – a harmless note, for he reproached himself more than anyone – then he went downstairs, and then . . . Well anyway, Sandra and the hotel valet kept their secret pretty well. Acre hadn't given them away, so it wasn't hard. But mother nature has a way of digging things up that ought to be securely buried. Three months later Sandra found this out. Small wonder she kept right out of the way for a time. And when she did reappear, she had an 'adopted' son, Terence. And shortly afterwards she adopted another – to smooth out the adoption line with her friends. But couldn't she have said Terence was Marshal Acre's son? She could indeed : only no one would have believed her – she had been the only person on Long Island, busy as she was with her troubles and her tantrums, who didn't know the original Acre secret. That was the sort of thing Sandra had been letting herself in for all her life – she was so intense that she overlooked things. She couldn't overlook Terence, but she'd wiped everyone's eye quite cleverly over that one. . . . Proof ? . . . Well, what did you expect ? As it happened a look at Terence wouldn't tell you much. What else would there be ? The whole thing had been a confidence between friends (between Sandra and Uncle Bill), not a conference between lawyers. There probably wasn't any proof – and a good job too.

And there you had it. A plausible tale, perhaps, but not plausible enough ('erratic', Mr Chynnon had said, 'but not lubricious') for anyone to believe. Not plausible enough, then, for Mr Chynnon to buy. 'Great ones, her friends . . . excellent war record.' No : one would have to do better than that.


At lunch-time Esme received a note. It was unsigned, and merely told him to be in the gambling room of the main Casino at nine o'clock that night. He had been wanting to play the tables, and if he was going to be living in the Milton Road after October the first, he might as well have his fling. (Terence, who was intensely disagreeable about Maisie's sudden departure, could be sent to the cinema.) Besides, an anonymous summons ( probably, he thought, from the Duchess's voracious quest of the other night) was always an intriguing thing to receive. Meanwhile, he addressed himself to the task of soothing Terence. He and Maisie had had quite a night of it, because shortly after Uncle Bill had visited Terence's room, he had passed out once more and left everyone a perfect wicket. Maisie had been a bit surprised to find him in bed when she eventually got back to their suite – and still more surprised when he let her have it the next morning. But she had been swept off happily enough, and much too early for protracted liaison with Terence. On the whole, then, Terence's anger was not directed at Esme. But it was a full-time job cooling him down, and it was with a very deep sigh of relief that Esme finally pushed him off to one of the many American films that were showing in Biarritz.

Getting into the gambling room was an elaborate business. Esme's passport said 'student' of all ridiculous things (why the hell couldn't he have had the sense to put 'gentleman'?), and the word 'student' bears a very dubious connotation on the Continent. He had to explain, first that an undergraduate of Cambridge University wasn't a sort of hybrid between 'worker' and 'intellectual', then that he himself was an ex-officer of the King, and finally, when neither of these worked, that in any case he had been elected a fellow of his college that spring and had not had time to have his passport altered. It all went to show that the truth is far more double-edged than any fiction. Once again falsehood had brought him through.

The first thing that struck him on his entry was the atmosphere of excitement. He didn't have to have a drink or purchase a single counter : wave after wave of excitement swept through the room, wave after wave of that excitement which springs from hope fulfilled, hope deferred, hope in the midst of desperation, hope, above all, prompted by the second oldest instinct in man – avarice. At some tables men and women sat solidly with lists on which they recorded each number that came up, occasionally risking a counter in support of their researches. At other tables, people hovered, backed away, pounced back from a last minute bet, shrugged their shoulders, rushed off to buy more counters. A woman stalked from table to table, flinging down thousands of francs at once, and turning back to another to discover her gains or losses. An elderly man, with a great pile of plaques worth 20,000 francs apiece, covered the board with them, lost the lot, covered it again, won much of it back, covered it a third time. . . . And everywhere Esme looked sat the black, imperturbable, figures of the croupiers, bending over the tables like the gods overlooking Troy, quick and nimble, placing the counters, raking them back – click, click, wood against plastic – placing bets for the gamblers, paying, receiving, impervious. Like the chant of an overseer of galley-slaves came their regular intonation, 'Merci, M'sieur – pour les employés', as a lucky gambler tossed over anything from 100 francs to five thousand, 'Merci bien, M'sieur – pour les employés, pour les employés, pour les employés . . .' It was the background rhythm for the devil's own tune.

And what a tune, thought Esme. It was as stirring as a march, as alluring as the sirens' song, as sinister as the second movement of Beethoven's Seventh Symphony. He was not the one to stop his ears to it. He went up to the exchange counter. The minimum stake was 100 francs – about two shillings, he supposed – capital was necessary, you could never win without ample resources, it was not the moment to skimp. He put five thousand francs down. That should see him through for a bit.

He took his place at a vacant chair. The cloth was being covered rapidly. What did one do? . . . Yes, that was it, one backed an even chance for a bit and double when it lost. A hundred francs for Manque. 'Rien ne va plus . . . trente-six, noir, pair, et passe.' Two hundred francs then . . . 'Vingt, noir, pair et passe.' Four hundred. . . . 'Le Premier, noir, impair, manque.' That was it of course – seven hundred down, eight hundred back. One for a long chance then – nine. 'Faites vos jeux.' Nine. . . . 'Vingt-sept.' Start again. Manque. Manque it was – leave it there. Manque again. Another lost chance – nine. . . . 'Neuf, noir, impair, man- que.' The thrill went right through him. He had won practically nothing, three thousand five hundred francs perhaps, but he had won *en plein,* the gambler's dream. He had beaten the whole board. And now he would –

'Well, well,' said a voice behind him, 'the tutor making his fortune.' He looked up. It was Trito.

'Don't worry now, I'm delighted to see you do so well. Sandra sent me on early to see how things were. I can tell her they're prospering. . . . But come and talk a few minutes, my dear Esme, – roulette afterwards. Over here. But we must have more roulette – it's the best game in the world for character. That's the mistake made by our great public schools – football and cricket as train- ing grounds for life! They should install roulette : what can be better training than to see worthy people hopelessly ruined and worthless ones raking in a fortune? The way of the world in a pig's bladder! Far better they should lose a term's pocket-money in an hour, run into debt, win it all back in ten minutes. That'd teach 'em to go looking for absolutes all over the place, that'd see to their καλοκἀγαθία! A good lesson of παντἀ ῥεῖ – all in flux, my dear Esme – is what they need.'

He too seemed to have caught the excitement.

'And that was why I asked you to be here. It's an atmosphere for talk, tutor, we can say what we please on any subject here in the midst of roulette and baccarat. It's a purgative, an enema, παντὰ ῥεῖ if you take the joke.'

'Several thousand pounds worth of education,' said Esme, 'have been preparing me over the last ten years for just that sort of joke. But since you make such claims for the atmosphere, go on and say your bit.'

'Well then,' said Dr Fibula Trito without preface, 'you've now been doing this job for well upwards of a month. What do you make of it all?'

'You asked me that once before, and didn't pause for an answer.'

'I should like one now.'

'It's a great life but I'm weakening fast.'

'If you could be a little more explicit ...'

'On what particular points?' asked Esme.

'Well, take myself, for example. Am I your idea of the family physician and friend?'

'I think,' said Esme, 'that you're just a crook.'

'That's better. And what sort of crook?'

'A small-time crook. Do you want to know the details?'

'Certainly,' said Trito.

'Well, for a time your behaviour puzzled me. Or rather, it didn't while it was going on, but it did when I thought about it. Not that I didn't like it – quite the reverse. I looked upon you as an ally.'

'In what capacity? In the general one of cheating the rich?'

'Yes,' said Esme, 'but also in the more particular one, when I came to think about it, of extracting information from them which might possibly have an outside market.'

'Go on.'

'I thought that you, like myself, must be in the pay of a certain Mr Chynnon, who provided just such a market. I didn't know how far he was dependent on you, but I imagined to a considerable extent. And if this was the case, you couldn't have been telling him very much.'

'And what made you think that?' said Trito, raising his eyebrows.

'A list he gave me which was a most unsatisfactory document. It occurred to me that you had probably provided the information on that list – and had advisedly limited it to prevent possible competition from myself or, for the matter of that, anticipation on the part of Chynnon.'

'And what else, *stupor mundi*?'

'It struck me that your enthusiasm – for which I was very grateful – that Terence and I should come to Biarritz indicated your own inclination to follow us; and that it was therefore highly probable that you had some sort of a clue which led here.'

'But such deduction,' cried Trito; 'always pick a scholar when it comes to an affair of action. Their intelligence. But I'll tell you this much, scholar, you've allowed yourself to be misled. And who shall blame you? You've performed miracles with your data. But if you will allow me, I shall now supplement your data and destroy your edifice – or a great deal of it.'

'I should be delighted,' said Esme.

'Well, let us have two things plain for a start: first, my object is not information – at any rate not in the sense you mean; and secondly, there is consequently no question of a clue or a secret, in Biarritz or elsewhere – a point I shall expand in a minute. Let us then call my object "x". And let us add to this the fact that I am Mr Chynnon's doctor. You will understand then that I was not slow to hear about his little contretemps with our employer – in fact you might say I even helped to foster it: you will also understand that I knew enough about him to anticipate a favourable reaction to a little suggestion I had in mind. For my object, "x", required both money and cover: Mr Chynnon was in a position to provide both; and so, while in a sense *I* employed *him* (the reverse of your creditable surmise), at the same time *he* was paying *me* – or at any rate providing the money I needed. And how did I win him over? Simply by convincing him that "x" equalled blackmail: I wanted the information for blackmail, he thought, while he could use it for his own equally malicious but different purpose – denigrating poor Sandra, that is to say. He would receive all the information I gathered, and was to do certain services for me in return.'

'Rather a breach of blackmailer's etiquette,' said Esme, 'selling information to two parties.'

'Not so fast, tutor,' said Dr Trito: 'I did not say "x" *was* blackmail, I said Chynnon *thought* "x" was blackmail. If he thought I was capable of such a breach, so much the better for me and the worse for him. Because in fact there is no information and so he will receive none – though his money and his efforts have had their uses. But to continue. Chynnon obviously wanted to have something to chew on : so I devised a little fiction (with a factual basis) which I called the Acre secret. You will know by now that there was indeed a Marshal Acre who married Sandra and whose suicide was rather sudden. But since a detailed enquiry at the time and sixteen years of subsequent speculation have not elucidated the point, every sensible person concludes that there is no point to elucidate. Still, it seemed to make Chynnon happy. I gave him a non-comittal list of Sandra's old friends that made him even happier, and he even offered a substantial bonus should the secret ever be uncovered.

'Now it was about this time that I decided that "x" would require a further assistant for its completion. After a glance at your situation, I decided, my dear Esme, that you would do. It was a risk to employ you before observing you, but this was essential because you had to become actually and swiftly implicated in a fair measure of villainy so that, when the time came, you would hardly be in a position to object to giving your services. At the same time you could be observed by myself for suitability while you were, as I hoped, busy implicating yourself. It was necessary you shouldn't suspect me of observing you : and so here was another opportunity for Mr Chynnon to provide cover. Of course I had to find a reason to give him for wanting you included in our little plot; so I pretended to be convinced of the necessity for a constant inside observer : and of course you were treated to the Acre story in the hope, on his part that you might unearth it, and on mine that your interest in it would lead you to get sufficiently enmeshed in iniquity to assist in "x" when the hour came. Chynnon of course agreed that it was as well you shouldn't know my part in it all till I had had a chance to observe your activities – though of course the end I had in view was very different to his.'

'Wasn't he surprised when you suggested an assistant – a possible competitor for the Acre bonus?'

'Not particularly. The bonus was a small matter compared with what he presumed I should stand to make by blackmail.'

'Do you suppose he would have paid what he said for the secret if there had actually been one?'

'I dare say. He's a vain, vicious and unstable man, totally lacking in any sense of proportion.'

'Hm,' said Esme: 'and do you consider that I'm sufficiently hedged around with evil to be enlightened about "x" and compelled to assist with it?'

'On the whole, yes. There are those notes to Chynnon. I could produce them, *as his doctor*, and stand by him in alleging they were forced upon him by yourself after your own suggestion that he might care to hear anything you could learn.'

'A little thin.'

'But I've no doubt of your acceptance, my dear Esme. Perhaps I had hoped you'd become a little more involved. But you'll be getting a fair reward – not quite up to the Acre myth standard, but still very fair.'

'But what about your insistence on Biarritz? You say no clue leads here. What is there about "x" that makes Bi—'

'A good deal. Many places would have done as well – Deauville, Le Touquet, Cannes – but Sandra herself suggested Biarritz, the Duke of Panton was a sure attraction –'

'Very well then,' said Esme, 'now we're getting to the point. Hitherto I've been busy being "observed" and becoming implicated. Wasting my time in fact. So you've observed me, you've trapped me, you've found me satisfactory: you've finally got us all to Biarritz, which "will do" as well as Deauville or Le Touquet; and now, I presume, you're at last ready to tell me just what your "x" game is and how we're to set about playing it.'

'It's almost depressingly simple.'

'Well?'

'Has it not occurred to you that Sandra may spend a lot of money here?'

'It has – I've already spent a lot for her.'

'Which is all to the good. And has it not occurred to you that in these days it's a criminal offence to spend a lot of money abroad, and that certain people are interested enough to pay very highly, I say very highly, for evidence that may –'

'Really,' said Esme, 'I honestly think this is the dirtiest trick I ever did hear of. You propose –'

'Yes,' rapped Trito, 'and I don't want any nonsense out of you just because you've been duped into following a dud line of –'

'So I have, have I?' said Esme, stung to the core of his being, 'I'm so stupid, am I, that I'm the only person living – or almost –

who knows there actually *is* an Acre secret, which is admittedly worth about tuppence, and WHAT IT IS?'

'Well, well,' said Trito, 'choose a scholar every time. You interest me, I must say.'

'Well, I just wanted you to know. It's worth a heap of scrap iron, but there it is. There's not a shred of evidence of course.'

'And you'd care to divulge it?'

There was one thing Esme could never resist – the chance to tell people how clever he'd been. All his vanity and all his love of telling a story rose to meet Trito's question. Step by loving step he traced his enquiries, his doubts, his perplexities; his find in *Caprice*, his luck with the 'Luritania Supplement'; his hopes, his fears, his expenditure, his final coup with Uncle Bill. If there was to be no thousand pounds, there would at least be a round of applause. He sat back after the final disclosure about Terence's parenthood, and beamed with self-satisfaction.

'Well, well, well,' said Mr Trito, 'I must say it's the most creditable piece of work. Who'd have thought it. Choose a scholar. . . . Well, well.'

'But you see what I mean – no sales-value?'

There was a long pause.

'No, I suppose not. But really, Esme. . . . Now let's think . . . Yes. . . . I wonder . . .'

'Meanwhile I suppose I'd better hear what you've got to say. Though I must say, picking up titbits is one thing, but spending a person's money abroad and then acting as an exchange stooge . . . You must admit.'

'No, no, my dear Esme, now don't go and hurry me. It's possible. . . . Well now, listen. You've heard that I required your assistance. Here is the position. I've been thinking about this for a long time, I've observed Sandra abroad, I know what her resources are. I also know that as things stand at the moment she'll have almost no francs at all except the customary allowance. I know, for example, that her account with a certain Paris dressmaker – an account she likes to pay regularly – has now been outstanding for much longer than usual. I know a lot else. And what it all adds up to is that she's now at a very low ebb for francs. For you, Terence, and herself the allowance comes to a hundred and fifty pounds worth. Of this, you've got about fifty for expenses – right? And just how far do you suppose the rest's going to get her, in Biarritz of all places, and with a hotel bill (what with you two and herself) that would knock a horse down? Furthermore she's a rare one for baccarat – she can't resist it, she loses often and heavily.

'Now what will be the result of all this? Evidently she will have to get hold of more francs – friends, the black market, anywhere. And it doesn't particularly matter where, because in every case it's a criminal offence. Are you with me?'

'Up to my neck in dirt,' said Esme.

'Don't be pert. Now then, where do you come in? You come in, my dear Esme, where I walk out. You will readily understand that neither my practice in general nor my position as Sandra's doctor in particular will admit of any suggestion, any suspicion however slight, of my being the agent of such proceedings. I therefore propose returning to London before Sandra even gets here.'

'That's sweet,' said Esme, 'that shows real professional tact. And so I stay here, do I, do all the dirty work, and end up as a notorious figure in a currency case while you make your fortune?'

'If you pause to think for as much as two seconds,' said Trito, 'you will realize that your position, both for incurring excessive expense and for collecting the evidences of it, is absolutely unrivalled. Furthermore there is not the slightest need for you to incur the least suspicion – Sandra is coming here without her secretary. Who is it then who will fetch and carry, haggle over the bills, collect the receipts, cash the travellers' cheques, be at her arm in the Casino? Answer me that.'

'Little Alf,' said Esme.

'If you like the sobriquet – little Alf. And what is required of little Alf? Very, very little. All I am asking of you is to get hold of bills, receipted or otherwise, and to try and remember the rough amounts Sandra disposes of at the Casino or elsewhere. But it is the bills that matter. Everything else – everything in the least bit dangerous or compromising – will be handled by me in London. All you have to do is get the bills – even one would be sufficient, provided it totalled more than the joint allowances of you three. This alone would be proof that she had exceeded the just amount – by however little. And it would not be difficult to establish that she had spent more money than merely on her hotel bill. Did Chynnon talk to you in terms of an act of justice?'

'Yes.'

'Then how appropriate was his wording! The wheel turns, a little twist is given, and back we are where we started – performing "acts of justice".'

'He also spoke in terms of hard cash.'

'I was coming to that. Now the thing is this, my dear tutor. It was my original intention to offer you a small sum of money – say £100 – for your services. But I do feel that the outstanding, the miraculous ingenuity you have shown – though admittedly in quite another matter – entitles you to the satisfaction of receiving direct reward for your perspicacity. It will save me a little money, so that I can afford to take a generous view, and will bring you a considerable benefit. In short, I have something far more valuable than £100 to offer you – on receipt, that is, of the documents I require.'

'Oh!'

'You have justly remarked that your little discovery, as it stands, is tantamount to worthless. But suppose I was to say I had a letter in my possession, a letter I had never previously thought of much account, but which I now consider might raise your expectations from the merest shadow to the most solid substance? Suppose I was to say that?'

'I should ask what sort of letter it was.'

'And I should tell you. "This is a letter," I should say, "written to me by Mrs Fairweather when she first became worried about Terence's behaviour. It would be untrue to say," I should add, "that this letter says anything concrete, but for one who knows as much as yourself it says everything by implication." You see, my dear Esme, she felt I should know – and how right she was – as much as possible about the boy's background – and also something about his parents. Very good: an adopted mother generally knows a little of such things, and it is evident she only knows a very little about the father. "Rough . . . vigorous . . . of the servant class" – that sort of thing. But when she comes to the mother, such is her zeal in the cause of a cure, she gives details way and beyond anything you could normally expect an adopted mother to know. I was surprised at the time, I remember. Now I am no longer surprised, only grateful. For in the course of ten pages she gives an accurate and detailed analysis of a woman who can only, given what we know, of a woman, I say, who can only be herself.'

'It seems rather a question of the hen and the egg. I mean, if you accept the story you'll take the letter as proof; or if you had reason to read such significance into the letter, you'd accept the story. But if you started with scepticism towards both. . . .'

'Chynnon does not start with scepticism. He starts with an almost superstitious belief. The mere idea of documentary proof will throw him into a trance.'

'And how successful do you suppose he'll be when he starts circulating the story?'

Trito shrugged.

'I don't know that we need trouble very much, you and I. The letter, like so many of Sandra's, has no heading, and luckily, in this case, no vocatives. If he finds himself thwarted, he'll get into one of his states, and I shall make a handsome fee. If he gets away with it, poor Sandra, what with her other little troubles, is going to require my constant attention. A remunerative appendix, you might say, however the story finishes. And do we make a bargain, scholar, a bill for a letter, and thus breed two acts of justice out of one?'

'Since, as you say,' said Esme firmly, 'I am trapped in any case, I feel I have no choice.'

'Irrefutable, scholar, irrefutable. And not a trace of pertness. But after all this talk of justice, we must have a change of idiom. Back to the tables, Esme, and the nice disregard of the wheel for all moral worth.'

# XVII

The next morning Esme inaugurated a new programme.

'How would you like to live in a suite?' he said to Terence.

'There's no harm in it,' said Terence, who was still by way of being disagreeable.

'Well guess who I met last night, and thinks it a good idea?'

'It's your story.'

'Trito. He's coming to have lunch with us and then going back. Your mother sent him to see how things were. He thinks things would be better in a suite.'

So they moved into Uncle Bill's suite at eight thousand francs a day.

'What do you say about giving a little dinner-party for the Duke and Duchess? After all, they're great friends of your mother.'

'It might be fun.'

So Esme arranged a dinner-party for six at a cost of five thousand francs a head.

The party was a great success. The Duchess shrieked, the Duke boomed, Terence found a new friend, Esme rediscovered an old one, they drank a toast and broke the glasses, and three of them fell through a sheet-glass window. Luckily they were on the ground floor.

Then they went to a night-club the Duke knew about, took Terence and his friend home, went to the Casino, lost all the money they had with them, went back to the night-club the Duke knew enough about to get credit at, and finally arrived home at four in the morning. And at eight in the morning Sandra arrived by the night train from Paris.

She appeared at the door of their suite with what looked like a regiment of assistant managers behind her.

'What's all this about a suite?' she said.

Esme slept in the room by the door. When he had woken slowly up he sat up in bed and gaped.

'*Sandra*,' he said, 'I didn't think – '

'I don't suppose you did. What's all this about a suite?'

'It was Dr Trito's idea. He thought we should have adjoining bedrooms.'

'So he thought that, did he? Did he suggest a private beach?'

'No.'

'Well that's something to be thankful for.'

Sandra then occupied Esme's bedroom. She unpacked, bathed, changed, and told the regiment of assistant managers to find Esme a servant's bedroom on the top floor. Then they had breakfast and went out shopping.

Shopping with Sandra was always rather fun – even more so in Biarritz. She bought everyone a present and a great many presents for herself. Sandra got a kick out of giving presents.

They stopped at Cartier's and bought a locket. Then they went to a photographer's to have a photo taken of Terence to put in the locket. The photographer was booked up for the morning, so they drove in a taxi to St Jean de Luz – which was big enough to have a photographer but too small for him to be booked up – and had it taken there. They paid treble to have it developed on the spot. It was too big to fit in the locket, and when they cut it down a bit Terence's forehead looked even more criminal than usual: but if it was cut down the other way the dent in his chin had to be left out, which Sandra couldn't bear. So finally they had to go back to Biarritz and make an appointment.

At Lanvier's Sandra bought herself a bag. Half-way down the next street the strap came unfastened.

'There's something wrong with this strap,' she cried.

When they went back to Lanvier's the manager showed her how to manage the strap, but even then it kept coming unfastened, so finally she threw the bag at a beggar out of sheer temper. It was a lucky day for him, because she had forgotten there were still ten thousand francs inside it.

'Where's Uncle Bill?' asked Sandra at lunch.

'He just went away,' they said.

'Most unlike Bill to change his arrangements so suddenly. He's such an old woman these days, too.'

'I think that's why he went away,' said Terence.

'At all costs,' said Sandra, 'we must play golf. I shall borrow the Duke's clubs.'

'Your Grace,' she wrote to the Duke, 'will you please lend me your golf-clubs. This is very important as I particularly want to try this course. It's most *urgent*, Your Grace.'

The clubs arrived – all except the wooden ones. The Duke said Sandra's temper was too uncertain for her to be lent valuable wooden clubs. But the irons were put in the corner and treated with the reverence due to the Cenotaph for some days. It always seemed to be too hot to play golf, however, so eventually they were sent back.

'Everybody,' said Sandra, 'goes into Spain. Esme must go to the Spanish consulate and get us visas.'

This was quite easy, but their passports had to be left there to be stamped. When Esme returned after lunch with Terence and Sandra, the consulate was shut. Esme had failed to notice that it always shut at two o'clock.

'It'll take more than this to beat me,' said Sandra. She knew as well as anyone else that by tomorrow the mood for going into Spain would have passed.

'Where,' she said to a gendarme, 'does the Chancellor of the Spanish Legation live?'

It took some time to get there and his house was shut. Somebody came and said everyone was having siesta. Apparently it took a thousand francs to rouse the Chancellor from his: and even then it was only his wife who was roused. She came down buttoning up her skirt.

Sandra said her husband was dying in England, and that she must therefore have their passports immediately. Her husband, she added, was a 'milord Anglais', a quaint touch which pleased Esme. The Chancellor's wife said the price for opening a Spanish consulate after two o'clock was five thousand francs. The Chancellor then came down and said that for the wife of a 'milord Anglais' it was ten thousand.

They all drove to the consulate. Somehow the word that the consulate was to be opened had gone round, and the place was besieged with haggard Frenchmen who all wanted emergency visas because friends or mistresses the other side of the border were either dying or had been put in prison. The Chancellor unlocked the door, admitted Sandra, slammed the door in everyone else's face, handed over the passports to her and received the ten thousand francs with true Spanish courtesy.

After which they went shopping in Spain.


One night Sandra and Esme went to the Casino.

'I think that man over there's an exchange spy,' said Sandra.

'He's the Duke's new secretary,' said Esme.

'He might still be an exchange spy.'

She played for a long time : whenever she had a 100 franc counter handy, she tossed it to Esme to use for roulette, as hundred franc counters are no good for baccarat. Nor, in her case, were any other sort. She came away poorer by fifty thousand francs.

'Now,' she said, 'we shall have to look at the bill and see how long we can stay.'

Esme shuddered.


'But you mean to tell me,' said Sandra the next morning, 'that you've almost used the whole fifty pounds worth of francs you were given? It didn't occur to you that a lot of that would be needed for the bill?'

'It did,' said Esme, 'but Trito said I must amuse Terence in every possible way – show him things, take him round the places, give parties for him.'

'But, Esme, whatever am I to do? I've just seen the hotel manager, and what with the suite, your parties for Terence, hired cars – the bill's going to be about a hundred and eighty thousand francs. That's thirty thousand above the basic allowance for all of us.'

Uncle Bill's dinner had turned the scale.

'Well,' she went on, 'your fifty pounds – that's fifty thousand francs – is gone, mine's gone in the Casino – and we're left with only fifty. The manager's busy seeing if he can't deduct a bit – mercifully I knew him in the old days – but even then . . . We shall have to go to Paris and arrange it all there. Now be a dear, and go to the desk: say we're leaving tomorrow morning and that I want the bill as soon as possible.'

Esme went to the desk. Really it could hardly be simpler. 'I want Mrs Fairweather's bill,' he said, ' – in duplicate.'

# XVIII

Early in October, Esme had one of the Bursar's dismal notes: Would Mr E. S. Foy call at seven o'clock on Wednesday?

'I must say, Esme,' said the Bursar, 'this is really very gratifying.'

'Yes,' said Esme, 'isn't it?'

'You've paid your entire debt to the college, which was beyond my wildest hopes, and – '

'And all my other debts,' said Esme smugly.

'But how did you manage it? Did Mrs Fairweather take a fancy – ?'

'Not exactly. I was lucky in the Casino, in a manner of speaking.'

'But however lucky you were, you couldn't bring much money back as things are now.'

'You mustn't interpret too literally,' said Esme, 'there are ways and ways of being lucky.'

'Evidently there are,' said the Bursar rather acidly.

'But another thing,' he went on, 'I must tell you that for once in a way you've done us all credit. I've had a letter from the solicitors that expresses great satisfaction, and another one from herself that says how very favourably Terence has developed and what a great help and comfort you were when things began to get difficult. I gather she's now in rather serious trouble?'

'I'm afraid so,' said Esme, 'her doctor tells me she'll have to take an extensive rest-cure after it all. In fact he's so worried he proposes accompanying her.'

'Well, let's hope she's in good hands. But to continue: she's so favourably impressed by your manners and general competence that she wants to put both her boys down for this college. What do you think of them?'

'Well, the younger one – whom I saw little of – is incredibly nice but rather stupid. The elder one's a good buy on any terms – he's extremely intelligent and, as she says herself, coming along nicely.'

'But what about all this "anti-social" business?'

'I think,' said Esme, 'that people exaggerate a little. There might have been something in it once, but he seems very friendly now.'

'Where's he at school?'

'He was in Switzerland. However, this trouble of poor Mrs Fairweather's has led to the currency people refusing her the special allowance for this purpose. So now he's been sent to Hadley Field – the headmaster's rather a snob and thinks it's a leg-up to have someone that's been sacked from Eton.'

'Well there you are,' said the Bursar, 'I shall certainly consider the matter very favourably. And now, Esme, about yourself. You seem to have emerged with credit and advantage from this business. I think you've been very lucky – undeservedly lucky.'

'I don't know about that. I was kept jolly busy, you know.'

'It still seems to me a small penance to pay for all the trouble you've given other people – and all the money you've spent.'

'I've paid it back.'

'That's not the point. There's a moral somewhere in all this,' said the Bursar desperately, 'if only I could find it.'

'There are a great many,' said Esme, 'but I'm not sure they're very much to your taste.' He rose to go.

'One more thing,' said the Bursar; 'I think you might just tell me what you found in the Casino?'

'A moral,' said Esme, 'though you might not call it that.'